THE
CAMBRIDGE PAPERS

A Novel About Love, Romance and Deceit

L. A. Wiggins

AuthorHouse™
1663 Liberty Drive
Bloomington, IN 47403
www.authorhouse.com
Phone: 1 (800) 839-8640

Published by AuthorHouse 05/29/2015

ISBN: 978-1-5049-0480-3 (sc)
ISBN: 978-1-5049-0481-0 (e)

Library of Congress Control Number: 2015905144

Print information available on the last page.

Any people depicted in stock imagery provided by Thinkstock are models, and such images are being used for illustrative purposes only. Certain stock imagery © Thinkstock.

This book is printed on acid-free paper.

Contents

Prologue

The briefing by General Thibodeau, my former ASA (Army Security Agency) boss in Frankfurt (who was now with the CIA working inside the London Embassy) was, I thought, a gift of an easy assignment. It was handed to me, along with a commission, because of past covert successes. However, this was no ordinary spy assignment as it was to begin as soon as possible in the British Isles. At least that was going to be tamer than previous assignments, which had involved crossing into a hostile environment and evading the East German Stasi (secret police) along with their KGB handlers.

There were several communist recruiters inside one of the world's most prestigious universities. Prince Charles was attending Cambridge at the same time, which caused me some concern. I would have to dance around the British Secret Service agents protecting him, which was going to be awkward for a CIA agent trying to expose traitors.

Inside Cambridge's hallowed halls were Marxist faculty members who had targeted the brightest students to indoctrinate them into their dark ideological world. When their mind games failed, promises of good marks were the tools. When these efforts failed, embarrassing accounts and photographs of sexual, drunken or drug-induced liaisons were used. I was asked not to stop this subversive behavior, but to take names and profiles of future civil servants who could have influence inside our own government. One has to keep in mind that subversives in Cambridge would not use guns and daggers most of the time; however, they would try to use logic, popular clichés and other psychological means to persuade their young, captive audience to forsake Western values or ideas.

A clandestine undercover mission had to be executed to improve past errors of the USA foreign services. The unbelievably traitorous acts done by the infamous Cambridge spy ring in the 1950s was never going to be tolerated again by the Americans. The extent of the damage from these evil men was not discovered until recently. Saying that our once trusted British cousins in the home office were embarrassed was an understatement.

These sleeper cells from the past were nested inside the British Embassy in the States, while pretending to be our friends on one hand, and stealing valuable documents with the other hand. British consulates in other countries were also infested by like-minded adversaries. Their goal was to do us as much harm as possible by stealing nuclear and rocket propulsion blueprints to give to their Russian masters.

My assignment was to become a part of the student body and gather plans on how future operations were to be carried out by a few pawns. There were no time restraints put on these young sleeper cells, who would collect their pay packets for years until they were instructed to hand over prized classified material. These agents would fester inside the British Civil Service and Foreign Office for a decade or more until needed. My job was to join them at their own game by pretending to hate capitalism, and at the same time be a friend and a fellow hater of Western ideas.

Setting the operation up would take several months; and finding the right house to operate from, close to the center in Cambridge would be an important task. The communist lecturers were instructed by their Russian handlers on how to sway certain weak privileged students into compromising situations. Most of these children had a parent who was a member of Parliament or parents who were part of the gentry, with their titles handed down to them over the centuries. Some of the weaker heirs would be formed into a tool to be used in the service of the KGB. Unfortunately, these traitors were protected by the old boy network.

Future services would be required of me before and during the school year. First, I'd work a covert operation inside the CIA training facility and then one behind the Iron Curtain, around the Christmas and New Year's holidays. Making liaisons with Czech and East German ladies was part of a strategy for keeping me safe. Unpremeditated murder while protecting one of these ladies was necessary to keep her from being raped by a Russian officer and two Czech soldiers.

Chapter 1

London CIA Briefing

Arriving in London on the day of my discharge from the Army, I felt excited and was in a euphoric frame of mind. I found there was a message at my girlfriend Nicola's house in Harrow from General Thibodeau. There were instructions for me to show up at the American Embassy the following Friday for a 10 a.m. meeting. Nicola's parents thought this was strange since the message was left the day before I was to be picked up by them at Heathrow Airport, and I was supposed to be a free man from the United States Army.

It was fortunate the message was rather vague. However, that added to her parents feeling that there was much more left unsaid. The need to call back was not mentioned, which was again suspicious and added to their confusion of who William Wright really was. The expressions on their faces were of the big question: How did the embassy staff know their house was where I would be staying?

The feeling after spending a few wonderful days with Nicola walking around Harrow on the Hill a free man, and not needing to report back to the barracks in Mannheim, was hard to describe. The next step of reporting to the embassy was of my own choosing. When I arrived at the London Embassy on Friday morning, General Thibodeau was waiting downstairs. He escorted me to his office, where another agent by the name of Joe West was also waiting to brief me.

Joe West and I didn't exactly hit it off as he seemed to think he was the cat's meow. When they divulged that they knew of me moving into a bedsit in West Harrow the following week, it was disconcerting to say the least. The need to listen and not act surprised was a way of telling them I knew they would find out eventually. That seemed a big deal to Joe and spoke volumes. They were certainly keeping tabs on me and my girlfriend.

"Wright, I am being transferred back to Washington. Joe here will take my place and subsequently be your contact now in Europe. You will be available for any ASA assignments when needed, answering to General Neuhofer when you are assigned to them. Agent West will now ask you a few questions. Is there anything you want to say?" Thibodeau said.

"Yes sir. I would like to start by asking for a commission since I will be unofficially still in the Army. My request is for a rank of captain and the pay to go with it."

"I do not see a commission being granted Wright, a captain's rank is out of the question. How about second lieutenant to be offered in June?"

"I will compromise down to a first lieutenant, sir."

"Okay Wright, I do not see a problem with your request."

Evidently agent West did not agree by the look on his face.

"Joe, do you have any questions for agent Wright?"

"Yes sir, Mr. Thibodeau. Thank you for the chance to interview this agent. Billy, can I call you Billy?"

His question was meant to be condescending so as to get a negative reaction from me in front of a high-ranking CIA operative. I wanted to play his game since I was put on defense, I would run with it. That would clear the air so to speak. I did not like Joe West because of his behavior in the past in Prague. I thought that I had better answer quickly before he had a chance to pile it on.

"Yes sir, I am honored that you would like to call me by my first name, Joe."

"Billy, I would have kept you a non-commissioned officer until you have proved yourself to me."

"Thank you, Joe, for your bluntness and being honest. I like a person who is forthright. It was good that I asked agent Thibodeau instead of you for my commission. Joe, you know all about my assignments in Prague and Leipzig. If those successful actions didn't impress you, then I don't have a hope in hell to ever please you. We can call it quits and I will walk away from the ASA and the CIA."

Joe said, "You will stay and listen for now, your reputation precedes you Wright as a protagonist with no regard for your superiors."

I responded in a low, controlled voice, "You sort of fancy yourself, Joe, with your lack of respect towards a fellow agent, especially when he is the one being sarcastically assaulted in a confined area."

Thibodeau with a smile interrupted the prickly exchange between West and me by saying, "No one is going to leave or quit as long as I am in charge. I would like to see you, Wright, by yourself and you, West, wait outside until I call you; your behavior is unacceptable in front of another agent."

We waited until West left the room for our private conference. Joe was fuming as he slammed the door behind him, probably to show his dissatisfaction with the CIA director keeping me on the payroll.

Thibodeau started with a lecture that sounded a little like a high school dean would give to an offending boy, "Wright, I would like for you to show more respect towards West. He is going to be in charge, with me giving guidance to him from our Langley Headquarters."

"Sir, may I speak truthfully about my past experiences with agent West."

"Wright, it would be unfair to disparage West without him being here to defend himself."

"I understand, sir. What I have to say can be said in front of him if you would like to call him in."

"Wright, I know West to be an arrogant so and so, and what you have to say would fall on deaf ears. I will send you my office and personal phone numbers when I am settled in my new post in the States. You will answer to me through West. I will tell him about our conversations. Now before you go, one last request. I want you to tell me everything that happens here in London, be careful of other agents, especially West."

"Thank you again Mr. Thibodeau for my promotion, and I will do as you say and communicate with you at least once a month."

"You are excused lieutenant; expect to hear from us in the next two months."

Everything was out in the open now as I shook the general's hand. As I was about to leave Thibodeau stopped me at the door to tell me that he would like me in Washington in June for a two-week training course.

"Let me know the date sir, and if you could give me a couple weeks notice it would be helpful. I would like to give the commissary warehouse at least that amount of time, so they could find a replacement."

West did not like the rapport Thibodeau and I seemed to have. I finally left with the thought that working with West was not going to be a lot of fun. I waited at a small park around the corner for Nicola to join me for lunch at a local pub.

Nicola showed up and saw other Americans sitting on benches eating their lunch. She wanted to know how the meeting went.

"It was a good, informative sharing of ideas. Let's try the pub on the corner. I am starving, how about you darling."

"Absolutely famished Billy, you seemed to be on edge, is something wrong?"

There was no need to tell her about the dust up at the meeting and while we waited for our meal it was unfortunate that Joe West happened to come through the door with a rather suspicious-looking character.

I asked Nicola, "Please don't say anything right now. Watch those two men who just walked in and let me know your opinion on how they look and more importantly how they handle themselves."

After she finished her wine I said, "Please get us another drink Nicola, and have the barman put it on my tab. I would go if it wasn't for those two men; one of them might recognize me. The dark hair gentleman is a bit of a skirt chaser and I don't want him to follow you with his eyes over here. He knows me and I would like to study him for a few minutes."

After 10 minutes Nicola was back and said "Here is your drink Billy; now you must tell me what this is all about."

I said, "One of those men will be my new contact. In this morning's meeting we were at odds with each other. I know some things about his past that I find unpalatable, and he finds it uncomfortable that I seem to know."

"Nicola, tell me your opinion on the appearances of the two gentlemen and the way they are conducting themselves."

"I feel like a spy darling, isn't it exciting that we are so close to the American Embassy, those two could be spies. Is this what you do when you are in other countries?"

"Yes, now study those men for a few minutes and let me know, as the English would say, about their deportment."

I waited a few minutes while finishing my lunch for her summation of agent West.

"Darling, the dark-haired American looks a little shifty by the way he cannot relax. The heavy gentleman is definitely not British, maybe Russian, with his ruddy complexion and large pitted face. His hair is oily along with the worst cut imaginable as his hair bristles out from the side of his head."

"Great observation Nicola, now remember what those two guys are wearing. One suit is from Mayfair and the larger man's suit looks as if it were bought from the secondhand market. With your major being in art could you make a sketch of the larger man? I am quite sure we will see those two again before the year is out."

"Now think of this very carefully over a few days. Would you like to join the intelligence community? You could help me or be my assistant; we will be able to spend a lot of time together."

"I will think about it darling, but I do not believe so. I'd rather be a school teacher."

"Wise decision. When they get up to go, I want to follow the Russian and see where he's headed. Wait a minute! The two men are getting ready to settle their bill. Let's see who pays. The Russian is paying, that is not a good sign for the Americans. Russians do not do something for nothing; I have learned that in my briefs with the ASA. Follow him outside to see if he is walking or riding."

Nicola came back in to tell me the Russian was waiting for the bus.

"Please go back outside and ask the taxi on the curb to wait for us. I will be out as soon as I settle up the bar tab."

The bus had just stopped as I went outside. Nicola was already in the large black London taxi, wondering what I wanted to do. With the bus slowly pulling away I asked her if she was sure the man got on the bus.

"Yes, he is on the bus," she assured me.

The taxi driver opened his little sliding window and asked, "Where to Guv?"

"Follow that bus please and stay back far enough so the person on the bus doesn't get suspicious we are following him."

"Yes Guv."

Nicola was staring at me with a look of disbelief. She probably thought she really picked a right one this time. Of all the prospects she could be engaged to, why did she have to pick me. I had to think of something to say pretty quickly.

"I am sorry about this Nicola, but there may not be another opportunity like this again, to gather needed information. This may be a wild goose chase, but I don't think so. Please let me do this, and I will try not to involve you again darling."

I caught a glimpse of the taxi driver watching me in his rear view mirror. He quickly turned back to watch the road.

Nicola was looking uneasy and said, "Billy, I am a little scared with you doing this. Everything will be alright, won't it?"

"Yes, Nicola, don't you worry. I need to see where he is going for my own well-being in the future."

The driver was still occasionally studying me through his rear mirror. Now it was time to assure the driver I was not a bloody crackpot.

I had seen the name of the driver on his registration pasted on the glass of the partition separating the front compartment from the passengers.

I asked him, "Kenny, if you would let this play out I will make it worth your time. Take this 20 pound note to go towards your fare."

He said in his heavy Cockney accent, "That's a lot of dosh me old cock. It won't be as much as 20 quid, Guv."

"Give me your business card and you can apply what is left over to the next time I use your taxi. Can I call you in the future when a taxi is needed?"

"Right you are, Guv."

"Billy, I have never known anyone to pay a taxi fare in advance! It is not what we do in London," Nicola said.

Kenny looked at me as I winked at him. He laughed out loud and said, "Don't worry, love. Your man is different, but as far as I can see 'e will do you right, even if 'e is a Yank."

She blushed as she smiled and nodded in agreement. The driver had now stopped again 50 yards behind where the bus stopped. We saw the man get off.

I said to the driver, "Wait a minute, that's our man in the old brown suit. I need to know where he is going."

"I know, Guv. I've picked 'im up several times. This is my turf, I was born several streets back of those first row of flats. 'E really isn't a bloke you two want to be seen with, a real villain."

"Do you know his name?"

"No mate, he doesn't natter much; I reckon he's a miserable old so and so and foreign. He doesn't bloody well tip, either. One can tell 'e's been in a few barneys. I once seen a shooter sticking out of his vest."

"Looks like he may be going into that building on the left Kenny; he is looking around to see if he is followed. I need to get out to see if there is a name on the bell box."

"You youngsters stay put. I'll 'ave a look. If 'e cops me I'll ask if 'e rang for a taxi. I 'as me notepad ready in case 'e gets jumpy."

The taxi driver walked brazenly up to and through the door. I thought to myself that this man may be a godsend in the future if I needed to watch this Russian and Mr. West. Kenny seemed to have very few boundaries or he had ice water flowing through his veins,or maybe he's a spy looking to keep track of what I'm doing.

Nicola nervously asked. "Billy, I feel this is an invasion of that poor man's privacy."

"Nicola that poor man is most likely a Russian KGB agent. You heard Kenny tell us he in his way of putting things. He is not a nice man. What in the world is a barney?"

Nicola, giggling and saying at the same time, "A barney is slang for a fight the Cockneys use. They have their own language here in London; they all seem to drop the 'h' in most words while in conversation."

Chapter 2

My First London Contact

Kenny was back in the cab. "Right mate, 'is name is Volkov, the cleaning lady says. She doesn't like 'im because 'e isn't a nice man. 'E leaves vodka bottles on the floor every day and seems to drink often when 'ome. She's alright, that lady who does the cleaning."

"Thank you Kenny for getting his name for me. Can you take us to Baker Street Station; we are looking for a place to have dinner."

"I'll take you to my local where the food is first-rate."

After a five minute drive he said, "We're 'ere now, you two 'ave a good time; it's been a pleasure, Guv, and you've been a little different clientele than normal, I'll say."

"Will you join us for a meal?"

"I 'll 'ave a pint if you don't mind, and then I will 'ave to get 'ome to the missus."

The name over the door was 'Flanagan's Pub and Restaurant.' The little hotel next door was called 'The Sherlock Holmes Hotel.' It was amazing to be in this area of so much history, and we soaked it all up.

The barmaid was glad to see our driver as he asked her to take good care of us since we were his friends. I felt good that he would say we were more than just a fare.

Over the beers, I was setting Kenny up as a contact without actually asking his permission. Nicola was now getting into this cloak-and-dagger stuff. Kenny also was asking questions about why we wanted to know where Volkov lived.

Not wanting to answer his question, he turned his attention towards Nicola; he reckoned he knew some friends of one of her mother's sisters, from working in London during the war.

Nicola said, "Yes, all of mummy's family is from around the old Kensal Green area."

Before he left, I asked him if he could pick me up at the Piccadilly Circus Station the next morning.

"Sure mate, give us a bell on the old blower as the time you will be there. My missus takes me calls. Give us your names and I will make you two a priority any time you need a ride. Write down your names for me to give to 'er indoors."

When he left, Nicola mentioned about going with me again to watch and stakeout a place. I assured her that 90 percent of stakeouts were very boring.

Kenny was correct. The food was great and we were given song sheets, with all the patrons singing Irish melodies while we ate and drank.

We caught the tube back to Harrow where I let Nicola know I would be out all the following day, and would see her in the late afternoon.

Right on cue Kenny was waiting outside the tube station at the arranged time.

"Good morning Guv, where we going?"

"I would like to see what Volkov is up to today. There is a cafe across the street from his place. How about a cup of tea and a full English breakfast while we watch for him to leave?"

"Suits me Guv, me missus said it was too early to fix me breakfast. In the past, on occasions, I would take your geezer and drop him off at a Hyde Park entrance."

The waitress took our orders and brought us a large cup of tea to start. The heavy blue-striped cups looked different than ones you would associate with in an English restaurant.

I had to set up a payment for Kenny, in case he had to wait with me all day.

"Kenny, I need to know for now and in the future how much you need for a day's wage."

"Right Guv, 'ow about a score for the day."

"What is a score?"

"Twenty nicker, Guv, or 20 quid. I see what you mean, Guv, not knowing the slang. We 'ave several interpretations for every type of note or coin. This will be your first day of Cockney learning. Now 20 pounds as you now know, is called all of the before mentioned names. Hold on, Guv, your geezer has surfaced; we better pay the lady and get ready to follow him. I will see you in the motor."

Once in the taxi, we were waiting for the Russian to hail his own cab. I kept quiet to see how my driver was going to play out this setup. With the Russian cab moving Kenny waited to make sure it wasn't going to make a u-turn.

"Right, Guv, we're off. I reckon he is 'eaded to the park, we will see."

"Okay Kenny, you know what to do. Here's the 20 quid. If he gets out at the park, leave me and I will call you later. I need to be at the American Embassy around 4 o'clock, waiting outside to watch for an acquaintance of mine who should be going home then."

"Right you are. Where are we meeting up if you decide to stop at the park?"

"I will meet you a block from the embassy. Park up with a good advantage so you can see the front door. If my hunch is right, we may have another passenger."

"Right Guv. They 'ave pulled over and your man is settling up with 'aving a natter with one of my mates driving that cab. I'll see what the geezer's game is."

"Thank you Kenny. I will see you later on."

As I followed the man through the gated facade, I turned around to see Kenny parked side by side with the other taxi. I thought, *how wonderful is that; having someone work for me who knows all the back streets of London like he does*. I let Volkov get 100 yards in front so if he turned around I could not easily be seen.

This was a large park where one could walk on the paved paths or on the grass lawns. I chose to follow him at an angle to make sure I would not to be even remotely seen a long way behind him. He seemed to be in a hurry as he wasn't stopping to see if he was being followed. Did that mean someone may be tailing me while I stalked him? With paranoia sinking in I walked quicker to close the gap between us, and past a large tree that I could double back a few yards to see if I was also being watched.

As I peered around the edge of the giant tree, I saw another suspicious-looking character walking in the same direction as Volkov. Now I had to shadow him, and keep the Russian in sight, just in case he wasn't part of the meeting. I must say he did fit the caricature of a spy, with his ugly brown suit and a heavy, dark trench coat.

The Russian walked to the left of a narrow lake with a wide paved walkway. He joined another man on one of the many benches fronting the lake. It was strange that he didn't pick an empty bench, unless he was meeting this man. The other suspicious-looking man joined them. The original person on the bench had his back to me, and was wearing a hat and a tan overcoat.

I pulled my camera out of my coat and took a picture from the rear. I had to make my way around to their left since the lay of the lake slanted to the left. Still 50 yards away I angled my walk over the grass field, occasionally stopping to take a discreet photograph.

Darn, they started walking away from the bench and each other. I took a number of snapshots hoping one would be clear enough to distinguish their features. This was an old 35 millimeter camera I had bought in Germany three years earlier. It still had its original brown leather case, and I had my fingers crossed hoping the camera would come through.

Not wanting to take any chances I decided to follow the man in the tan overcoat. He must have been foreign because the winter wear in London was still dark clothes, even though it was April. Now it started to rain, making the man walk quicker, back towards the park's large entrance.

The man entered the underground station and proceeded towards a waiting train. I walked onto the car behind him while keeping visual contact. There was a discarded newspaper on the next seat, which I used to hide my face.

At the first stop he got off and made his way to an escalator that went down almost 100 feet, then to a ramp where his next connection was. There were hordes of people shuffling around and waiting for a train, covering every inch of space.

I snapped several more photos of this guy at different angles. When we got to Grosvenor Square tube station he got off. I stayed on the train with my camera aimed towards him from my seat. It was evident he was an American national going to the American Embassy.

Later on Kenny was waiting for me down the road from the American Embassy, and I got into the back of his cab.

After conciliatory greetings he said, "I need to go for a Jimmy Riddle if that is okay with you, guv."

"Yes, go see Jimmy; I will stay here, we have plenty of time before most of the embassy staff leaves for the day."

He was laughing as he walked towards the public lavatories. Then I realized; it was Cockney for going to the bathroom. I must have seemed like a fish out of water here in London.

When Kenny got back he said, "Now then Yank, this is your second lesson on the use of Cockney verbal-isms. A Jimmy Riddle is used for going for a piddle." We both were amused by his sense of humor.

Chapter 3

Going Around West

Getting back to business I said, "Kenny, I need for you to do something for me. I will be working another job for the next three months with weekends off. This job of mine will be on the outskirts of London, and I will be unavailable during the day.

"While you are working this part of London, will you be agreeable to keep a log on the people like the miserable foreigner Volkov? I will try to post some photographs of another two people of interest that need to be documented. This is only if they frequent your taxi. Like you said before about the Russian, these people are not to be trusted no matter what. If they happen to find that you are watching them, I need for you to become invisible to them until I am back towards the end of June. I will certainly understand if you decline, but I will still like to have the use of you and your taxi."

"Yes, Guv, I think I can keep your log. They won't 'ave an inkling I am watching them. Can you tell me what this is all about Guv?"

"I am an employee of the American Embassy, and only two people in that building know of me and no one else. One of them I trust, the other one is a little suspect."

"Do you mean one of them is a prat?"

"Yeah, I guess he is, if you mean he is unsociable."

"Here is 50 quid Kenny, which will have to do for the time being."

"Guv, that is mighty generous of you, thank you very much. Do you 'ave a number where I can call you on the blower."

"No Kenny, I will call you on most Saturday mornings."

Thibodeau just came out of the building and was walking our way; he held his hand up to hail this taxi.

"Bloody Yanks, doesn't 'e see my flag is not up? Sorry Guv, I didn't mean you."

"Yes, you did Kenny; however, you are mistaken. I am a Johnny Reb, not a bloody Yank. Go ahead, let him in; I need to have a powwow with him."

We both laughed.

"I like you Guv, you are straight up."

Thibodeau started to apologize to the driver for not seeing his cab was not in use, and was shocked when he saw me in the back.

"Get in sir, where do you want to go?"

Thibodeau was still taken back but managed to say, "Wright, what is going on with you being here today?"

"I needed to see you without West guessing what I was up to."

Kenny started the taxi's motor.

"Kenny, stay put for a few minutes." Thibodeau looked even more concerned with having the taxi under my command.

The man in the tan trench coat came out of the American Embassy and onto the sidewalk walking the other way.

"Go ahead slowly now, Kenny, I want to have a good look at the man there in the hat. Don't look at him Kenny; I want Mr. Thibodeau to tell me who he is."

"Now wait a minute agent Wright, I must protest at your very unusual behavior."

"Alright sir, I can explain. First, do you know who this man is?"

"Of course I do."

"Mr. Thibodeau, is there any place we can go to have a quiet talk?"

"I would suggest my house, but now I don't think I want you to know where I live."

"Sir, you are understandably taken back by my actions. I assure you after our talk you will feel quite differently."

Kenny joined in, "That young man is alright, 'e is."

Thibodeau was staring at me and shaking his head with disbelief.

He said, "Alright, tell your cohort to go to Mayfair Gardens. I live around the back in the smaller apartments."

Kenny was listening and gave his interest away by answering him.

"Yes Guv, I know where exactly you live."

"Oh great." Thibodeau started to laugh, and patted me on the back as he shook his head again.

"This better be a good meeting, Wright, or you are out of the system forever. Let me tell you, your record of insolence doesn't do you justice."

Thibodeau instructed the taxi where to stop.

"How much is the fare? I don't see a meter."

"Taken care of Guv."

I told Kenny I would call him next week. He waved good-bye as he continued down the road. We could still here him laughing.

Thibodeau looked back at me as we started up the steps, and shook his head again. He rang the door bell to have his wife, I would guess, let us in. She was a nice lady, almost as round as Thibodeau.

We were left alone after the formalities, and were both handed a cup of tea. Mr. Thibodeau wanted something stronger so I ended up with both cups, as he told me to finish his tea also.

In the conservatory on the back of the house he said, "Okay Wright, this had better be good. I do not make a habit of inviting agents into my home."

"Yes sir, I know this is unorthodox to say the least. When I left your office yesterday, my fiancé and I went to a pub close to the embassy for lunch. While we were there, West came in and seemed to have a foreign agent meeting him for a drink. Afterwards, I followed the foreigner to his house along with Kenny the taxi driver. The man's name is Volkov."

"This morning I staked out his apartment and followed him past Hyde Park corner and deep into the grounds. He met with two other gentlemen; one of them was the same man with the tan trench coat that I asked you if you knew. Sir, do you believe that happenstance can ignite an answer or start one on in solving a problem?"

"What is the problem you are talking about Wright?"

"Well sir, on my third assignment in Prague, someone alerted the secret police to my whereabouts. I had to cut my visit short by a couple of weeks because of this unfortunate action by the Czech authorities."

"All of your assignments were successful. I wouldn't worry about it if I were you."

"That is the problem sir, you are not me. I have to take all precautions to guard myself from being found out, no matter where I am."

"I must say, Wright, you are blunt, bordering on insubordination, and

what does this have to do with West?"

"West, I was led to believe was the CIA agent in charge of Prague.

I had a problem with an agent that was a paid informant for West. She left the reservation and started working both sides of the street. I had concerns on the second day of my first assignment in Prague that she was a plant by the secret police. It is an instinct that I have of reading people, sir."

"Okay Wright, are you able to read me? What am I about to do?"

"Yes sir, you are torn between hearing me out or throwing me out, so you can get on with having your dinner."

Thibodeau laughed out loud, "To a tee Wright, to a tee."

He then called out to his wife. "Mother, fix another place at the table for a guest. Wright is staying for supper."

"Oh wonderful, Tibby, we seem to never have anyone visit anymore."

"Wright, wipe that smile off your face, and if you ever mention the name my wife calls me in the embassy or anywhere, I will have you thrown in some dirty dungeon in Scotland."

"I believe you would sir," I said as I laughed with him.

"Now, where were we? Oh yes, the trouble in Prague. This is just between us. West was appointed by the President to keep an eye on my boys in Europe, the paranoid so and so. I never did like or trust agent

West and from your reaction this morning, I feel he has left you with the same impression,"

"Let me get back to you on what happened today in your happenstance. I do know that I want you to start working for me outside of the embassy as soon as I go back to Washington," Thibodeau said.

"Sir, I am starting work at the Ruislip Air Base commissary warehouse next week stacking shelves."

"No you are not; you are employed by me as of this minute, if you are willing to hear me out now. The pay will be more than you would get stocking commissary shelves."

"I am a little taken back by your offer, sir."

"Okay Wright, this is the plan that was okayed by Langley yesterday. Your office will be ready by next Tuesday in the embassy, where you will have a place to use only when we have a meeting. It will be one floor under West's suite of offices. Now down to the unpleasantness of your new job. The man in the tan overcoat is the ambassador's liaison officer and his trusted protégé. The three of them went to university together and belonged to the same fraternity. They are as thick as thieves and not to be trusted. I want a report on them every week since you have discovered a problem with the people they associate with," Thibodeau said.

"I will be leaving for the States at the end of next week, so we have little time to set the ground rules, and for you to get embedded in the embassy and fully operational. I am taking a chance by allowing you to share my secretary and having access to this office, especially with your need to gather information on who you consider to be friend or foe," he added.

"Now Wright, can you trust the taxi driver and how much are you paying him?"

"He has come up trumps so far sir; however, I would never totally trust anyone one hundred percent if push comes to shove. He has already gone beyond the call of duty in an awkward predicament that I had willfully created. I paid what he asked sir, which is 20 pounds for a full day's work. I've learned some time ago when you haggle a price over a job you get short-changed in the end. When one pays a little more than the going rate, you get much more quality and quantity in the end."

"How much of a weekly expense do you think you will need? You will be guessing until you get into the job."

"I have no way of showing on paper how much the taxi is, as he works better with cash; and he knows the tax man may want to hear from me if he ever did turn me over. Seventy five pounds a week should cover the expense of the taxi and my commutes for now. When I go to Cambridge, the cost may go to 80 pounds a week. I would rather not show transportation costs as it would alert West and the embassy high ups to my contacts and movements."

"Okay, Wright, we will start you on 80 pounds a week expense; and if anyone asks for receipts you tell them they have to go to my office in Washington. That is a lot cheaper than your expense account in going to Prague. We never received any report on what that money was used for. West thought you were taking us for a ride, what do you say to that?"

"General, West is probably an expert on taking someone on a ride. I would appreciate the flexible use of the agency's money without having to spend countless hours filling out paperwork, explaining where every penny went. The allotted funds would be used to keep me safe or putting it bluntly, money buys loyalty with most folks in most countries."

"Wright, we will continue this conversation over supper as my wife is a very good judge of character."

While we were eating, Mrs. Thibodeau asked, "Are you from the South, Mr. Wright?"

"Yes ma'am, I was born on a small farm. Please call me Billy, ma'am. Your cooking tastes just like my mom's."

"That's nice, isn't it Tibby? We were both born and raised on a farm also, in Louisiana."

"Yes dear. Now Wright, let's get back to the double agent in Prague. She was never put into the ASA report that she should be removed."

"No sir, I thought it was best to give her a little more money than find another person who may have turned out the same. I can safely say the agent is working with us now and has been put to the test by me."

Chapter 4

Shadow Agency

After his third Scotch, Thibodeau was laying out his plan of using me to watch out for the agency's interest in London. His plan was a short range, one year covert action. It would encompass retrieving secret Cambridge papers and traveling back to the embassy to keep an eye on West and his cronies during the college midterms.

"Wright, you will have to excuse me if I start repeating myself. This set up is between us, no one else will know. If you get caught spying on our embassy guys, there is a good chance they will want to get rid of you once and for all. You could be accused of working for a foreign government. Do you understand that no one will help you? I don't mean to sound cavalier, but I will protect my future; and they will get you if you are not careful with everything you do," Thibodeau said.

"Remember they have your file to look up known associations, including your fiancé, her parents and friends in the UK."

"Thank you sir, for being upfront about that possible predicament I may find myself in if I am not careful. I need to have the dossiers you have on West, Volkov, the ambassador and the ambassador's assistant. I have to know the ground rules before we play this game."

"Okay, I will get you what I can before the end of next week. You will be told where the bodies are, too. What you do with the information is not my concern. When you call me in the States you will have to use a public call box. Do not use the call box out front; it is bugged by our team. Alright Wright, you will have to go now, I will see you Tuesday at 0800 in the embassy."

"See you then sir."

When I left, Kenny was driving by and stopped to ask me where I was going, which struck me as a little odd.

"'op in Guv, I'll take you to 'arrow."

"Thank you Kenny, but I can catch the tube."

"No mate, you paid for a day's work, I owe you some time. 'ow did it go with the general, Guv? We Cockneys like to use what we call aliases for our punters. Thibodeau will be the general and the embassy 'is compound."

"Sounds almost like spy code words to me. I like them Kenny. We worked things out after he threatened to get rid of me."

"Tell me Guv, what is your game?"

"You don't want to know, Kenny. You like going to sleep at night without wondering about some bloke outside, leaning against the closest lamp post in the dark, don't you?"

"Right you are Guv, we'll leave it at that."

"Plans have changed. I am not going away as planned."

"Right Guv, I will give you the bull's-eye back when we get to your girl's 'ouse."

"I guess 50 quid is a bull's-eye. Keep it and let me know when it's used up."

"Right Guv. Were 'ere."

"Thank you Kenny, I will call you next week."

Nicola's father came to the door as the taxi was pulling away; he waved to the driver.

Inside he commented, "That must have cost you a packet my son. Was that Kenny? We go back to the war; we were mates then, until we moved out to where the posh folks live."

"Yes, sir, that was Kenny. He's a nice guy."

Nicola poured me a cup of tea and started to get my supper.

"I already ate," I said, "tea is all I need."

"What have you done today?" she asked.

"My plans have changed. The embassy is calling Ruislip on Monday and telling them I won't be available. They want me to start working for them on Tuesday."

"That is wonderful news darling. Will you have to move closer to your work?"

"I will commute from South Harrow for a couple of months so that I can be with you, especially on weekends. Nicola, I would like to see you as much as possible."

"Now, thanks for the tea, but I need to get to the bedsit for some rest."

"Good night ma'am, sir," I said to her parents.

Nicola said, "I will walk you home darling."

"It's too foggy Nicola for you to walk outside. Let's meet up tomorrow morning for coffee at Wimpy Bar, and I will tell you all about today."

I needed some time to myself to digest what Thibodeau had proposed I should do for him. It would have been nice to have her company that night; but thinking about the next week was something that had to be played out in my mind, in a quiet setting on my own.

It would be worrisome to have Nicola walk back by herself on this pea soup of a night. It was difficult enough for me to pick my way through so many side streets. You couldn't see more than a few feet from where I was walking.

When I finally made it back, I could hear my landlord's television behind the closed lounge door. We communicated once a week, on a Monday afternoon when the rent was due. That was okay by me as I wanted to keep a low profile.

I met Nicola the next morning for coffee and explained the change of plan that Thibodeau had requested. She couldn't be told everything I was to be involved in as her safety eventually could be compromised. Later that day we shopped for a couple of suits and dress shirts in London. We stayed away from the embassy area, so not to possibly run into any of its staff.

We had a fun weekend together, and on Monday, Nicola was teaching school so it was a rest day for me. On Tuesday morning, not knowing the train schedules I left Harrow at 6 o'clock. Walking into the embassy at 7 o'clock with only the Marine MPs around was a little awkward, as I had no identification to show I was working there. They said that Mr. Thibodeau wasn't in, he normally showed up a little later. I was escorted to a waiting lounge on the ground floor.

When Thibodeau arrived, an MP must have told him where I was waiting.

He came in and said, "Wright, I will send for you in about half an hour; we will discuss what you have to do about getting registered to work here. It may take all day to get the paperwork in order. Wait here. If you need coffee or tea, the MPs will get it for you."

"Yes sir."

After about 30 minutes an MP came to escort me to an elevator where he entered a code and pushed the top button. He advised me not to wander around any other area since I only had top floor clearance.

General Thibodeau was waiting for me as the elevator doors opened.

He said, "My wife and I enjoyed your company the other evening. She found you to be a straight-talking Southern boy; she liked that about you. Now for your being here today, I have set up a coffee meeting at 9 a.m. for you to meet everyone on this floor and your floor, which is the next one down. You need to just listen and not add to any conversation, regardless of the context. The less you say the better;

it gives no one a chance to pick apart your way of thinking. You will be evaluated today by your words and the way you react."

An older lady came in to take me downstairs to the passport office to have my photograph taken. She then escorted me back to the director's office. While I waited outside the office, a nurse came up to take me back downstairs again to the embassy clinic.

After a physical and being asked about visible scars on the side of my stomach and on my right leg, the physician was satisfied that were no health problems. This had to be done quickly, since it was getting close to my meeting with the other employees.

Everyone seemed to know why I was in the embassy as I was escorted back upstairs, this time by a MP to a conference room. Everyone stood up from their chairs when I was led into the room. The only ones I had seen before were West and the man in the tan trench coat. That reminded me of the photographs to be picked up that week on Harrow High Street.

I was introduced by Thibodeau with him going around the table in order. Everyone was staring at me with a look an analyst would have studying a mental patient for the first time. West was the most curious, probably wondering why I was brought in off the streets so quickly. Little did he know he was one of the reasons for that.

The meeting lasted just over an hour and I was asked to have another discussion with West and Thibodeau in West's office. Walking into West's office was a waste of time since he was moving upstairs to the director's office, and we had already met there once before. I didn't have to look for safe or secured closets for obvious reasons.

West started the briefing with the niceties of meeting a new protégé. He was going over the same ground we covered our last time together. It still ran an hour of nothingness; even Thibodeau wanted to get out of West's office. We headed back to Thibodeau's office where he invited me into his chambers.

He said "Let's go get something to eat, I am famished. First, I have to get some of the agency's money out of the safe to pay for our lunch."

As he slid a carved panel over on the side of his large desk to get to the safe, I edged closer to see what the combination was. I suspected he wanted me to know anyway by the way he turned the combination lock and called out the numbers.

I excused myself by asking where the washroom was. In the bathroom I wrote down the combination to his safe and went back to his office.

When we got outside Thibodeau asked if my taxi cab was around. The funny thing was he was parked on the other side of the street. We went over to see if he was available.

Kenny said "'ello mate, I 'm waiting for one of your high ups, you know the dark-haired man. Mr. West I believe he said his name was when he was on the blower."

As we were talking Kenny flagged down another black London taxi to pick us up, one of his mates I presumed.

Thibodeau asked "I didn't understand one word the taxi driver said. Who was he waiting on?" When we entered the taxi Thibodeau gave the driver his address as the place we were going. "Mother is making our lunch, I need a drink and I am taking the rest of the day off. You have to go back to get your identification card and a key to the building this afternoon."

"He is waiting for Joe West, sir."

"I would like to know where West is going."

"That is taken care of sir."

"Is your taxi friend working the embassy staff for you Wright or was it as you like to call it a happenstance?"

"I don't know what you mean, sir."

"Cut the BS and drop the sir when we are out of the office."

"Yes to your question, and thank you for letting me talk to you as an equal."

"I thought so, and you are welcome to the second part." We both laughed.

In his house we were ushered back to the den by Mrs. Thibodeau, who had a pot of tea ready for us.

When she closed the door behind us he said, "You have two cups of tea to drink, I am having a large Scotch. You will let me know where West is going today, won't you?"

"Yes, did you find out anything about the meeting in Hyde Park with your two men and the Russian Volkov?"

"They were both questioned by another agent individually and denied knowing anyone called Volkov."

"I don't want to jump the gun. I may have photographs to show that they were with him."

"If you do we will both confront them and see how they react."

Chapter 5

Hooking the New Director

After catching a bus back to the embassy, I was greeted by Thibodeau's secretary at the entrance with my ID card. She explained how to swipe it, and where it logs in the time I entered a specific area of the building. She also briefed me on the other security measures that had to be taken, and gave me a key I had to sign for. I was told to take care of the other errands Mr. Thibodeau said should be done.

That meant I should go and get the photographs in Harrow; and after picking up the package from the developers, I was early enough to meet Nicola coming out of school. She was quite surprised to see me.

"Let's go for a drink in the pub; I need to look at some photographs that I took the other day. I will tell you all about it."

That was nice, getting away from work and meeting Nicola as she was about to walk home.

In the pub Nicola couldn't wait to see the photographs. Before going up to order our drinks I handed her the photos to have a look at. Chances were she wouldn't find them to be of any interest.

She followed me back with her eyes smiling as to say, *no one wants to see pictures of men talking in a park.*

Before sitting down Nicola asked "What am I suppose to be looking at darling?"

"Cheers! Boring are they?"

"Yes, you could say that. I thought they maybe of someone we both knew in Harrow."

"No, they are the Russian and two other men he met in Hyde Park the other day."

"It looks like some of these were taken from a train."

"I followed the man. I was curious about to see where he ended up and had to go on the underground train."

"So, where did he end up?"

"At the American Embassy. Are they clear enough to identify who they are."

"Yes, however, half of them are fuzzy and the men are indistinguishable, whereas the other half are good."

"Nicola, are you sure about not wanting to be a spy? We could work together following villains."

"No thank you, one such episode with you was quite enough for me, thank you very much. You do your spy stuff and I will teach school."

Going through the pictures, it was amazing that all three men were clear enough to make out. I was ecstatic that some did come out. I stuck them in my suit pocket. We left to go have supper with her parents, and then I was off to get some sleep for another early start.

When I got to the embassy early the next morning, my pass and key worked wonderfully. It was fortunate no one else was there as this gave me time to have a look around to see if any cameras were being used to survey the office.

I was in my office when Thibodeau arrived.

He came in and said, "Give me a few minutes. I would like to see you before anyone else gets here. We have to clear the air about your curiosity."

He continued, "You are on tape having a good look around here. I want to show you where the video cameras are, so next time you will be a little more cautious. I have erased the tapes before West sees them; he does not like you being on his staff. With knowing so little about you, it makes him paranoid. What he does know about you from your Prague assignments makes him uneasy as he thinks you are somewhat of a cowboy. He likes to pick his own team and you do not fit his profile."

"I am a cowboy and proud of it."

We both found that very funny as Thibodeau said, "Me, too, Wright."

"Thank you for erasing the tapes. I can't afford to be fired in my first week, sir."

"Wright, believe me, no one can fire you except me."

"Now for some unpleasant photographs for you to peruse, sir. I am willing to substantiate these snapshots in front of Mr. West if you desire."

"I would like you to be available if they say these are forgeries. If they admit lying to me when I asked them the other day, you will not be asked to come in. I really want these photographs for future use since they are on tape denying the meeting with Volkov ever happened. Do you have copies of these pictures kept in a safe place? Keeping your identity secret will be beneficial in having them guessing it could be anyone on my payroll looking after the interests of the CIA."

"Yes sir, I do. Sir, for my own interest, could you find out if the ambassador and his right hand man were ever exchange students from their Ivy League school and what foreign university, if any, they did attend. One last request is if any one of them manipulated a Rhodes Scholar grant."

"Will do Wright, you seem to have lady luck following you around, but do not get complacent because I know West to be not only a sneak, he can be vindictive. If he ever knew you had the audacity to follow him, he would get you back one day. That's a promise."

"Second thoughts Wright, I want you to disappear for now before these two men get here. I will meet you at noon at my house. Have your driver pick me up here at 11:45. What will you be doing from now until I see you at noon?"

"I will buy Kenny breakfast and go over the activities of Mr. West yesterday."

"Let me question your driver, I'd rather get it firsthand if West was being naughty," said Thibodeau.

"He won't tell you sir, I know him to be loyal."

"What impertinence Wright, are you the director now?"

"Not yet, sir."

Thibodeau roared with laughter, I thought he may have a heart attack with his belly jumping as it was. He motioned for me to get out with his hand waving towards the door. I looked back as he was drying tears that were leaking from his eyes. After closing the door he let out another loud roar. I had to hurry so West and his cohort wouldn't see me.

A safe distance away I called Kenny and asked him to meet me in the cafe across from his flat. I was ready for a full English breakfast without the black pudding and fried bread - chips would be okay.

Kenny was in the cafe by the time I got there with a cup of tea waiting for me.

"'ello Guv. Where we off to today?"

"Hi Kenny, I am grounded today. Can you pick up the general at 11:30 a.m. outside his compound, and take him home? I am meeting him there again for lunch. I will be in the phone box hiding, until I see you drive by."

"Yes mate, considered it done. You do get around in your tea break, don't you Guv?"

"Tell me about the man you picked up yesterday outside the general's office."

"Now Guv, I've never in my life seen such a more worried bloke. He met the foreign gentleman outside Victoria Train Station. I was instructed to take them to Cambridge University. After dropping them off I was told to come back in an hour and pick them up. What was I going to do in the middle of a place surround by fields of sheep?"

"Only the Yank showed up for me to take him back to London. He never said a word all the way back, not even anything about the miserable weather. Something funny is going on Guv with that bloke."

"The general will be asking you about this. Tell him everything you told me. This one is off the record, Kenny; no one else needs to be told."

"Right Guv. Now where are you off to?"

"I will be looking for a cheap bed sit or a place to rent."

"Nothing to rent in London is reasonable mate. I couldn't live 'ere if me and my missus didn't have a council flat."

"I need to familiarize myself with the city and the tube system just in case you aren't around some days. I will see you later in the week; thank you for your help Kenny. I have to go now."

I was back at Thibodeau's street a few minutes before 12 and saw Kenny drop him off at the door.

He waited to let me in. Kenny, looking in his rear-view mirror as he drove away, waved back at me.

By the time we were at the door his wife let us in. We headed for the den where there was a steaming tea pot and two cups with a drop of milk in them.

She said, just before closing the door behind her, "I will have lunch ready in half an hour; you boys drink your tea now and Tibby, Billy may not want two cups again."

He started to pour his Scotch but stopped to say, "Wright, I am leaving at the worst time possible, and you are going to be in the middle of a nasty transition. West went berserk thinking I had a tail on him when he saw the photographs. When he turned beet red I knew he was up to something he shouldn't be, and he wouldn't admit lying to me the other day. When he started to gather up the pictures, I told him to leave them on the desk. He left, slamming the door behind him.

"I brought the pictures with me knowing he would go into the safe to steal them. I will be called in front of the ambassador tomorrow for a friendly chat and I have seen this type of scenario play out in DC before. I really do not know how to handle the situation when I am asked to turn the photographs over. You seem to be quite aloof when pushed into a corner."

"When questioned, if it were me, I would say as little as possible. When you are holding a pat hand and cannot be beat, your opponent will bluff with a lot of talk. Your deafness will transmit an essence of confidence. Let the one digging himself into a hole keep digging," Wright said.

"If a smile makes the perpetrator even angrier, they will divulge more than they wanted to in the outset. When you get to your office tomorrow morning, put the photographs in a diplomatic pouch. Have your secretary address the package to Langley along with a diplomatic seal. She will remember such an unusual request," he continued.

"Take the package with you to the ambassador's office when you are summoned. What would it take for you to hand over the package? I would ask for your own man to be put in place as the new London CIA director. Remember who is involved. West is a throw away, the assistant ambassador being prosecuted will mean the end of the current ambassador ever working in a foreign office again."

Thibodeau said, "How did you work all of that out Wright? Darn, darn. Darn, you have just saved the European agency from going rogue. I have just the man in mind. The one I wanted before who is in Frankfurt, a certain general in charge of the Army security agency. I think you know him, you brilliant SOB! Lunch is ready, let's get washed up. We both will take the afternoon off."

His wife came to get us and saw we were on our way to the kitchen.

At the kitchen table he asked her, "Friday being our last night, how would you like to go out to eat? I would like to invite agent Wright and his fiancé to join us."

"That would be wonderful Tibby; we hardly ever go out anymore."

"Okay. Wright you choose the restaurant and the time. We will enjoy the ladies and not talk about business."

"Fantastic, sir. I have just the place for a good sending off. Kenny will pick you up at 7 p.m. so you won't have a late night."

"I will see you tomorrow at noon. Stay away from the embassy until then. You may have time to go to Cambridge to have a look around. Make yourself known to the fellow that hires out the punts. Without being obvious ask for Burt and tell him you were told he may have a job opening up, poling river boats full of tourists up the river. Now off you go Wright, I'll see you tomorrow."

Instead of going back home, I went by rail to Cambridge to see Burt for a punt up the river Cam. What a strange euphemistic term that was. I waited until all of the college kids working the punts, pushing tourists upstream, were gone before approaching an older man who could be Burt. After inquiring, he confirmed he was Burt. He agreed, after I spoke Thibodeau's name, that I could start work on July 4. It was his weird way of getting back at us for defeating the British.

He wanted me to buy him a beer with the agency's money. There were two pubs on the riverfront; he chose to go to the rougher looking one. We took our pints of beer outside in the chilly air where we could talk.

"Now then, how is the old goat?" he asked.

"He's fine. He asked me to get a hold of you so I could get up-to-date with what is going on. First, I need to know how much you are being paid, how often, and when was the last time that it was increased. He is having a problem with the new director coming in and does not want this conversation to go anywhere else."

He said, "You didn't tell me your name."

I replied, "My name is Ludwig."

"You don't sound like a bloody Ludwig. This place is a spawning ground for would-be Communists. The whole town is filled with bleeding reds feeding on our young darlings. Them Dons in their long fancy gowns are the worst of the lot outside of the occasional Russian. My measly allowance from the Yanks is 10 quid a month, and it has been for the last three years."

Chapter 6

The Cambridge Connection

I told Burt that I would be working for nothing and that would be his raise. I agreed to work two days a week. I would keep the tips for his and my beer money. He seemed to like that better than an increase in his allowance.

Burt was a likable straight talker. Unfortunately, he would speak without thinking first. I would have to remember that in case we were in a place that needed little discretion. The more beer he drank, the more vital information was freely given. Now with having a treasure trove of local information, it was time for me to get back to my digs in Harrow.

The next morning it was nice to travel to the embassy without hordes of commuters pushing and shoving their way into a rail car that could hold only so many people. I then knew where the term "squashed like sardines" came from.

I arrived at the embassy a little before noon for my meeting with Thibodeau.

His secretary told me, "Have a seat, he is expecting you and is on the phone."

It wasn't long before he came out into the reception area to get me. As I walked into his office he slapped me on the back and just had the biggest grin on his round face.

After closing the door he said, "Sit down my boy, it must be your birthday. It feels like mine because of you. Agent West is being moved back stateside; General Jerrald Ross Simpson, or JR, your old boss, is taking over. The ambassador's right hand man is still here. You were spot-on with everything."

"Sir, I never knew his name. I just called him general."

"He sure knew your name and wanted me to describe you. I said he is insolent, curt and damn near insubordinate. The general started laughing when I said that, saying 'to a tee Tibby, to a tee.' Oh my, we laughed until we cried over your forthrightness Wright. Now tell me, did you make it to Cambridge this morning."

"I went yesterday sir, after the scrumptious lunch your wife served us. It took several beers before Burt, the punt operator, opened up with the information I needed."

"I am going to miss working with you Wright. You have no need to keep me informed now that JR is going to be the new director. He is joining us for supper tomorrow night. He and his wife will be staying in our house for the night and they will move in next week. Now, where are we going for the meal?"

"It is a surprise, sir. You and your wife will remember your last night in London for a long time."

"Alright Wright, you can take the rest of the day off since you worked overtime yesterday. I will see you tomorrow night wherever your driver takes us. He will pick us up to go to the restaurant I take it."

"Yes sir. Will you be in tomorrow morning?"

"This is my last day. By the way, my secretary will gladly work for you and JR. I have a surprise for you also tomorrow night; you see, you are not the only one keeping secrets. Now go see your girlfriend."

It sounded like Thibodeau was nipping already. I wondered what kind of surprise he could possibly have for me.

I got back just in time to meet Nicola again, coming out of the school yard.

She said, "This getting to be a regular occurrence, I am not so sure Billy you have a job. Let's go to Wimpy Bar for a coffee."

"Nicola, I accepted an invitation to have dinner tomorrow night with the new director, and the old director and their wives, if you have no other plans, would you like to go?"

"That would be fine, Saturday night we have been invited to a party, which is the only commitment we have."

"Great, we will arrange to take the bus from your house to the station at 5:30 tomorrow evening then. I need to go home with you to make the reservations and secure a taxi for the directors."

"Oh, they get a taxi do they?"

"Yes, they do since their age is the difference. I rather walk with you holding my hand instead of being in a stuffy old taxi."

The next morning seemed quiet on the top floor of the embassy. Thibodeau's secretary, Miss Peabody, came in early to box up his files. I stopped to ask her if she was also finding it quiet. We went down to the ground floor to have a coffee in the cafeteria. She was forthcoming with anything I needed to know. I knew this would be a good working relationship.

She did thank me for helping to get rid of that creep Joe West. I thought then that Thibodeau must have confided in her a lot. We both spent the rest of the day boxing up and carting stuff to the freight area, where the boxes were to be loaded into a crate for shipment back to the States.

We enjoyed each other's company as we laughed and joked all day. I told her I was glad she was staying to help the new director. She reminded me that she was also going to be my secretary when I moved upstairs.

She then put her hand over her mouth and said, "Blimey, I wasn't suppose to let the cat out of the bag; it was going to be a surprise tonight at the restaurant."

"Thank you for letting me know. I will act surprised when I am told and you will be, okay."

"I would never be any good at that spy game; I am always letting the cat out early."

It was good to be going back home to get ready for the dinner date. Everything was arranged for Kenny to pick up the directors and their wives, and Flanagan's had reserved a table for six.

Nicola and I left on time and were at the restaurant 30 minutes early. We had a drink as we waited, talking about how we should act in front of the old boss and the new boss. After getting another drink, our group walked in with Kenny.

I got up and introduced Nicola to everyone with Kenny saying, "I used to know you when you were just a nipper. Your family and I go back to the war. I will leave you all in good hands and be back to pick up everyone in two hours."

Thibodeau asked the driver, "How much do we owe you?"

"It's been taken care of Guv, see you at 9."

Before sitting down Mrs. Thibodeau arranged the seating with me in between the wives, and Nicola was seated between their husbands.

I started to open my mouth as General Simpson put a finger across his lips and said, "Let it be Wright." We both laughed. This was an old joke going back to the Bad Aibling days. He told everyone about that episode and this seemed to put us all in a warm, friendly atmosphere.

Thibodeau called the waiter over for his drinks order, and told him the check would be paid by him.

The waiter said, "Sorry general, your drinks and meals are compliments of the house. We hope you come again when you return to our shores."

Mrs. Thibodeau started to cry and said, "Isn't that nice, Tibby?"

"Now, now mother, no tears tonight."

The waiter went to get the drinks and came back with a suit in a long clear plastic clothes bag with an officer's uniform in it.

Thibodeau got up from his chair to make an announcement. "I present this uniform to one of our newest Army officers, First Lieutenant Wright."

Nicola whispered, "I didn't know you were being made an officer."

The new director, General Simpson said, "If you two get married, Billy will be ordered to have you kept up-to-date on his every move. Is that clear Wright?"

"Yes sir."

"One more piece of news, come Monday you will report to the top floor and have an office next to mine."

I acted surprised and said, "I am so overwhelmed and do not know what to say in response."

The general blurted out, "Now there must be a first for everything."

We all settled down and as soon as we stopped talking everyone was given a sheet of music for a sing along. The meal was very good and the more Scotch Thibodeau drank, the louder he sang.

We couldn't believe how soon Kenny was back, telling us it is time to go.

We all headed for the door as Kenny said to Nicola, "'ave another drink me love, I will be back as soon as I got this lot home, and will drive you back to 'arrow on the 'ill."

We went to the bar to have another drink.

Nicola said, "Oh darling, what a fun night. You never told me they gave you a commission."

"I never thought it would happen this quickly. My pay has also increased to more than double."

Kenny was back and we were off to Harrow. We were both exhausted and went straight to bed since her parents seemed to be sleeping.

Monday came quickly and I was at the embassy at the same time as the new director.

He talked about how he and his wife enjoyed the celebration Friday night. When Kenny the taxi driver arrived at Thibodeau's flat the next morning to take them to the airport, it was an added touch of fate.

The rest of the day was spent with the secretary and me setting up my new office. As the general was in briefings all day and getting acquainted with the procedural process to enter the building, I was able to convince the secretary of my willingness to make this office the best it could be. I arranged for Kenny to drive us to Covent Garden for lunch, where Nicola and I had had cucumber sandwiches one afternoon.

On the way back she was nonstop talking. "I ain't never been taken out for lunch before, especially to a posh place like that, Billy. The only place me ole man takes me is to the local chippy on Friday night for a fanny craddick(haddock-fish and chips). That was a real fancy robin hood (good)," she said in her wonderful Cockney slang.

"I am glad you liked it."

I caught Kenny's eye in the mirror and his smile. Getting back to the compound I asked her to wait at the door for me.

"I need to settle up with Kenny."

"Won't be long, Guv before you are talking like a native, sort of speaking. Are you working her or are your intentions strictly business?"

"Business only Kenny. I am a one lady man. Besides, she's married or spoken for."

"I thought you were honorable, Guv. Be careful, she does favor you, I can see it."

"When will you be needing the motor again? I thought about taking the missus to Brighton for the weekend."

"It's only Monday, you do plan ahead Kenny."

"Have to Guv, in my business; not like you cloak-and-dagger blokes that never seem to take a day off."

"I won't need you over the weekend."

"Right you are, Guv."

"I may need you in a day or two for another trip to the country. I will give you plenty of warning."

"You know where to find me, Guv. Outside your building, most times."

Chapter 7

CIA Indoctrination

The past two months went by with setting up the Cambridge network, and finding a place to live where one could observe university activity. I had to wait for the perfect apartment to be available after the start of the summer break. That worked out, as I had to travel to the States for four weeks.

My contact at Dulles International Airport, just outside Washington in a rural area of Virginia, was waiting as I exited the customs area. It was a shock to see that it was Joe West. Ironically, he was my way to get into the Langley complex. In the car I felt trapped with this proven jerk, who then had the opportunity to interrogate me, with me having no way out. I feigned being jet lagged to avoid giving him information he wanted about London CIA operations, especially how General Simpson was working out.

West dropped me off at the barracks that was going to be my home for the next 25 days. After entering my room, Mr. Thibodeau was waiting for me. He put a finger across his lip for me to be quiet. He then pointed for me to go to the shower room where two chairs were set up. After closing the door and turning on the shower, he asked me to sit down.

He then said quietly, "I sent Joe to get you for a reason. Sorry about that. Did he grill you on the way here and what did he ask?"

"It was all about the London business and specifically JR. He wanted to know if everything was kosher. I didn't talk to him. He thought the jet lag was causing me to sleep."

"Good job. Now for the bad news; he is a lecturer here on covert operation techniques. What do you think of that?"

"It's a waste of time and taxpayers' money. Are any of the cadets experienced?"

"No Wright, they are raw. I am apologizing beforehand because your Cambridge duties are curtailed for the time being. You will get some good useful information from some of the other instructors; they may save your life one day or at least will give you an insight on how other agents work.

"This is important, West was able to handpick his training team and you must not be seen to be disagreeable in any way. West will bait you by asking, has anyone here served in the field, hoping you will boast and elaborate on your experiences.

"Another lead in will be asking if anyone here ever traveled to a European country. You must not divulge any experiences because the information you have in your mind belongs to the agency. He is working to get you kicked out of his classroom and out of the service. West is bitter about being expelled from London and his chance of being its director in charge of all spies in Europe. That would have been disastrous if it wasn't for your timely surveillance."

I asked, "Sir, are you and your superiors not concerned West may be setting up a new network of loyalist to him? How could this agent still be in the CIA?"

"That is the reason you are here, to find out who is behind the setting up of a shadow agency. You know how this works because you have done it yourself in Prague and London. Wright, I know you are surrounding yourself with safe people, are you not? You were able to have West removed faster than what you thought possible."

"Sir, I never looked at in that way. Yes, I do look after myself first and maybe the results are a product of my interest in keeping alive."

"I know it is, and that is why you are being trusted by a few individuals in the company with my recommendations to deal with West. The top 10 recruits in your class will be invited to do a six-month course on the farm. You are instructed not to be a willing participant in any exercises. If you are picked to extend your training regardless of your lack of enthusiasm, well that should tell you something."

"West is consumed by paranoia and suspects everyone he had contact with in England, even you Wright. Be aware of him when you are having a drink or a snack. Sodium pentathlon is still used for extracting information and can be administered in food or liquid. I have to go before this room is put on the watch list. Go and see if anyone is around by pretending to be looking at the sights. First, get your clothes off and put on the hotel robe. You just came out of the shower."

"It is all clear. Before you go, is the phone secure?"

"Nowhere is secure on this base. You would have to go back to the airport for a clean line. Even my office phone is suspect. Wright, good luck, I will not see you again unless it is here in your shower room."

Chapter 8

Retiring the Lecturer

We were all assembled in one of the agency's classrooms for the start of our course. The intro lasted until lunch, where we all started our own clicks or associated with the people we were attracted to in the cafeteria. I was studying West as I am sure he was doing the same with everyone. There was a strapping young recruit who looked as if he had just left the ranch.

No one was interested in sitting next to someone who looked rough, rangy and could have the smell of a steer. I thought the opposite: *He would be a better prospect than someone reeking of Aqua Velvet.* Maybe he would be a good candidate for someone to watch my back. We introduced ourselves and it wasn't long before he asked why I wanted to work with the CIA. I was vague, in case he was a plant. I turned the conversation back to him and his reasons for being there. What he was telling me was trivial and going in one ear and out the other.

At this time West was chatting up the prettiest girl in the class, and not paying attention to anyone else. She had captivated him and it was love at first sight or until his wife found out. The tall rangy ranch hand was intrigued by my ability to remember everything he said. Myself an ex cow puncher added to making conversation about wanting to work outdoors.

West was amazing, letting a 30 minute lunch break turn into an hour. I was then thinking who was going to be the sacrificial lamb back in the classroom for West to score points with, for the sake of the Doris Day look alike.

Back in CIA school, the first question was as Thibodeau predicted. A few students put their hands up; however, I did not, as he looked at me wondering why.

He asked me, "Wright, did I not pick you up at the airport off a flight from Europe yesterday?"

Everyone turned around to have a look-see as to who Wright was.

"Sorry sir, for not raising my hand, I was busy writing your question down."

"I see you are still somewhat of a smart aleck. You see, Wright and I have a brief history. He has been in the service for 20 minutes; I have been in for 20 years. His short stint was with the ASA, a sort of kindergarten compared to the CIA. Is that correct, Wright?

I thought quickly how to escape this firestorm without West being scorched. So what if I had to lie about my covert successes. After a long 10 seconds I answered him.

"No sir, I was an ordinary soldier and was asked to do a favor for Army intelligence in West Germany. I was not a success in the one thing I was told to do. I asked to go for training with the CIA so I could possibly go back to the ASA. You see, I am still unofficially in the Army and hopefully will be accepted to go onward."

"I have my doubts Wright about your chances of moving to the next stage."

It worked for him as Doris was impressed with his power to fail or pass a hopeful student. It worked for me as he was back in the driver's seat once again.

The next two weeks went by as boringly as the first day. It was so dull that it was a job not to fall asleep in class. The last week, with three days to go, West was in his element by announcing who stayed or who had to go back home.

On choosing day, West after his usual, "Good morning students," was prowling the classroom and said "When I call your name, please leave the classroom and go pack your bags. An MP is already at your room. Better luck next time. A taxi is waiting and you have one hour to leave or be escorted off the grounds."

Doris was all smiles. I knew she was going to be okay. Everyone else was stunned with his cold, blunt statement. That is how it is played, trying to get a reaction.

Knowing this was not a life or death situation and the fact that we were being filmed, added an element of curiosity to see how West handled his short-term power. He morbidly wanted to see what reaction all of us would have to a possible chance of failure, and the eventual death knell from his pointing finger.

The video was now running with the reactions being magnified with some type of zoom-in camera on each student as their name was called.

West started again, "Before calling out names, you will need to just look at yourself to see one of the reasons you were asked to leave. Now if you look at Wright he looks calm, no reaction, why? He doesn't care if his name is called. That is a face of a cold, unfeeling predator. I hoped he would have just flinched so I could call out his name first. However, I have time on my side to catch him out."

Everyone turned around, except Doris and the ranch hand. Their smugness spoke volumes as to why I was so calm as they were shocked at their own reactions. All but three names were called, me, Doris and another young lady. What a waste of time, but not for West, as he needed sheep for his network.

We were taken to the farm after lunch to spend two nights for a familiarization course. After less than an hour's drive in a large black Chevy Suburban, we were let into a military base. West left us with an orderly at one of the barracks to get unpacked and into our running gear. We were to jog and run over a five-mile course over steep and hilly terrain.

While going through his show-off stretching routine he barked out instructions, "Keep up with his pace or you will be left behind to find your own way back."

After 40 or so minutes Doris bent over and groaned as she fell to the ground. I thought *right on cue.*

The other young lady helped her up and was told by West, "Stay with her until a medic arrives. Wright and I will continue the run."

I asked West, "Sir, I have had training in certain types of cramps, maybe I should stay and massage her cramps away and the other student can run with you?"

The look on Doris's face was that of someone getting caught with their hand in the cookie jar. I knew it was a set up, but I didn't know the real reason why yet. It couldn't be so we could be alone could it? I also knew that West wanted to get back at me for the London episode. No, that would be too infantile even for this jerk.

He barked his orders out again, "Wright, you are going to run with me because at the top of the mountain it is treacherous, and we need to go with the old buddy system."

We started off on the flat with the terrain gradually getting steeper. I was wondering if we were to run five miles and back again or was it five miles round trip. This base, I was thinking, was quite large as after an hour of running we still seemed to be on government land. I started lagging behind on purpose to conserve energy, not knowing what his game was. Nearing the top it was treacherous with what looked like 100-foot cliffs and just a small trail that a billy goat would find hard to stay on course.

West had been out of sight for 10 minutes as I trudged on. Twenty minutes later I saw that he was lying on the ground about 20 yards in front of me. Not knowing if he was hurt or was waiting to even the score for me having him sent back to the States, I sat on a boulder so I could observe him. He moved his head in a way so he could see if I was approaching. This was going to be interesting to observe his intentions.

I slowly jogged towards him as if my breath was totally gone, gasping and heaving sounds to go with an unsteady appearance.

West was hoping to ambush me and as I within a yard of him I fell to the ground coughing, blowing air through my nostrils. I weakly asked if he was alright.

He leaped up with a large rock in both hands and said, "You are the one responsible for me losing my director's job, are you not? I will crush your skull if you don't own up."

I didn't answer so he would think I was still out of breath. The longer he held that boulder over his head the weaker he would become. I weakly waved my right hand and fell to the ground.

When I was back on all my knees and hands I whispered, "I know who it was."

He leaned over me with the rock ready to crash onto my head. I rolled over to the right sweeping him off his feet, as he fell backwards he lost his balance, still clutching the boulder. The heavy rock caused him to be thrown over the cliff without any hope of grabbing something to hold onto.

I could not see him from the path's ledge; he must have gone all the way down as nothing was heard from him or bushes being pulled out of the side of the cliff.

I hurriedly walked back towards the base and then started running for the last mile. I ran to the front gate where the MPs were, with me gasping for air and telling them what had happened; they called the officer of the guard so he could assemble a rescue team. The officer knew exactly where to go and it had to be done from the trail. A helicopter couldn't get down to the canyon floor.

I was told to go back to my room and get cleaned up. I called Thibodeau to tell him the sad news. He was out of the office and I was instructed to stay put until he could return my call. I decided to have a cold glass of wine in the bath to help cheer me up.

Thibodeau called at the wrong moment, as I was just getting into the hot soapy water. The glass of wine was already on the edge of the bath. When I picked up the phone Thibodeau started talking before I could say anything.

"Now listen Wright, do not say anything to anybody. Keep your door locked and do not open it for anyone, or make a sound until I get there. I will be with you within the hour."

He hung up the phone too quickly for me to tell him anything else.

Back in the bath there was a knock on the door by Doris asking if I was in, sounding like she was crying.

I didn't need to see or speak to her; it would have been hard to pretend that I liked West. Anyway, I was following orders and enjoying soaking the muscles that seemed to be protesting after all that running. I had to replay in my mind what actual happened several hours ago, for Thibodeau's report.

Chapter 9

West is Finished

Thibodeau knocked on my door as I finished getting dressed. The officer of the guard was with him, with his clipboard in hand.

Thibodeau acted concerned in front of the officer.

"Wright, do you need to see a doctor or any sedatives to help you cope with what you went through?"

"No sir, I will be alright after I have a lie down."

"Okay Wright, the officer will interview you in the morning. We will leave you alone and hope you feel better."

The officer of the guard understood and left the room. Thibodeau closed the door after the officer left.

"Sir, have they found him yet?"

"Yes, he has a broken neck and was killed instantly. Now tell me exactly what happened."

Thibodeau was shocked that West was going to make me confess and then kill me.

"These three weeks have been a total waste of taxpayers' money. At least we know now what West was planning.

"I don't think it was a total waste, there is one individual from the class who could be a formidable agent."

"Is it one of the two ladies West picked to go on with the training?"

"No sir, they were only conquests for West. The person I thought might be okay is a tall rangy fellow, who had just walked away from his father's ranch somewhere in Texas. He is a bit boring, with a deadpan look on his face all the time, but he's as strong as an ox and very agile."

Thibodeau nodded then said, "I am taking you out of here tonight. I have called for an ambulance to take you to Walter Reed Hospital where I will meet you and put you up in the Hilton. We need to call that rancher as soon as possible. You may have to make the call since he knows you. Is there anyone else we could use?"

"No sir. Anyone West liked, as you know, would be weak. He dismissed every one of the men to cut out the competition for the girls. He only wanted me so he could obtain valuable information on the London investigation. He was upset at my finding out about his peccadilloes in Prague, especially with one of his informants, Andrea. Who, incidentally, passed his dispatches over to the Russians.

"His goal was to eliminate anyone who was involved in London, and eradicate them just in case they were involved in his dismissal. I am sure you would have been eliminated in time. I do believe he would have kept a journal somewhere to tick off all of his adversaries if and when they were murdered."

"You may be right. The ambulance is here, now act as if you are out of it so the MPs won't be suspicious."

The ambulance went straight to the Hilton's back door loading bay; it was one of the firm's own men and vehicle. They put me up in a suite that had everything, including a wet bar and snacks in the fridge. Thibodeau followed up an hour later with all the papers from West's office. I was to go through all of his notes to find where the bodies were buried (bodies was code for secrets). He assured me the room was secure. He was also sure my phone calls would not being listened to.

He said, "Put those papers away until tomorrow. Now pour me a double of the 12-year-old Scotch on the bar. Sure beats Langley barracks, doesn't it Wright? You are the luckiest man alive or the best agent we ever had. What is it?"

"Pure luck for sure."

"I knew you were going to say that, you BS artist!"

"How about me calling the rancher? I called him Clint after the Western guy, Clint Walker. He was really down when he was told to get out of Langley. Here's his number."

The phone rang. Someone answered. "Hello, who's there?"

"It's me Wright, from Langley, is this Clint?"

"What do you want Wright? It's late, I have to get up early to feed the live stock or my daddy will have a fit."

"I called up to see if you still wanted that CIA training class."

"Quit fooling around, you know I do."

"Call Delta in the morning and a ticket will be at the airport for you to fly up here on Monday."

"I will see you on Monday then. Thanks."

"Not me, I will be back in London on Monday. Now remember, you owe me. Your training will last a year, don't quit on me Clint."

Thibodeau said, "He owes me, not you, Wright."

"By the time he is trained and ready to pay up, you will be sitting on a beach in Florida."

"You may be right, I hope. I've got to go; mother has my supper on the stove by now."

As soon as he was out the door I couldn't wait to see what was in the papers West had in his safe. I read and made notes until 2 a.m., until over half of the papers were read. Too tired to carry on, I thought tomorrow would have to do, at least I'd broken the back of it.

Thibodeau called early wanting to meet me at the Hilton breakfast bar. One thing he didn't need was a buffet line. His wife had him on fruit and oats for his morning meal.

When I got downstairs his tray was already loaded up and he was walking towards his table.

I walked past him and asked, "Anything left?"

"They are bringing out more in an hour. I will let you have a piece of toast."

As I sat down I remarked, "I thought Mrs. Thibodeau had you on a diet."

"Don't you start! I get enough of that advice at home."

We both thought his remark was highly amusing.

"Sir, I will have the Joe West paperwork finished by lunchtime, if you could get me on this evening's Pan Am Flight to London I would be grateful. I would like be back in London tomorrow morning."

"Sounds good, Wright. Schedule your briefing for 1500 hours. You will still have plenty of time to make the flight."

"First class, sir."

"Very funny Wright, you're lucky you're not going home in a box. I know you are itching to go get started. While we were having breakfast a photo copier was installed in your room, a dairy for you to fill out with fake names and phone numbers and a Bible for you to read. Put your briefcase in a piece of luggage so they will find the West papers after you check in. Lock both cases to make sure they think you are being careful. Make copies for me and carry with you your notes only. If they do their job, you will be stripped searched in one of the airport security rooms. In the Bible you will find half a dozen blank pages for your notes in the middle of the Psalms chapter. Put the Bible in your luggage, and keep the names in your head for safekeeping."

I couldn't get away from Thibodeau fast enough to again go though papers of West's known associates. I started two lists: One for his London contacts and the other one of his college fraternity members, who were then in the Secret Service or were staff in embassies around the globe. The first on the list was going to be the Russian agent Volkov, and the ambassador was a close second. The suspense was building, who had he colluded with in London? He must have had an order from someone.

When I got back to my room, there was an MP buck sergeant standing by my door.

I asked him, "Sergeant, what is this about, and how long are you going to be outside my door?"

"Until you leave, sir."

I had a feeling he wasn't going to give me any more information. I would be wasting valuable time trying. First priority was to make copies of everything, even scraps of paper.

After five hours everything was copied, jotted and memorized. Now it was time to see if I remembered all of my notes by writing them down in chronological order: A - Ambassador's associations, B - brothers of the band (fraternity) and so forth.

A large SUV arrived to take me to CIA headquarters for the briefing with Thibodeau. The

MP guard outside my hotel door also went along, I guess to make sure no one stopped us.

The briefing was in Thibodeau's office with a man I was introduced as the director, with no name given, which seemed strange. He was a tall, lanky man with a New England accent. When I saw him, he reminded me of a character in early Dragnet shows. He had a dark, receding hairline similar to Joe Friday, but much taller. His profile would be hard to forget, especially with his large dimpled square jaw.

The director, not smiling, was all business. When the briefing was over, Thibodeau was cautious about getting into friendly chitchat with square jaw in the office. I was told to wait back in the foyer until my ride to Dulles International was ready.

After waiting for a half hour, I was getting nervous about making my flight. Square jaw walked by without saying anything, nor looking as if he even recognized me. *Okay,* I thought, *he wasn't going to get my vote for the most personable guy I ever met.*

Thibodeau came out of his office to say my car was waiting downstairs. He told his secretary he was seeing me to the airport.

When we were on our way he asked me, "What did you think of the director; and before you answer, he approved of the way you handled the West situation."

"You know me sir; I don't like to talk about the personalities of other people."

"Enough said, Wright. You are highly thought of by him, he may not show or say it; he is all business. He does know of your history and your successes. He thinks you have a rare gift and could be a good agent when you mature physically and behaviorally. Now don't take it as a negative opinion, it's all business. In his mind, he is the quarterback and it is his way for better or worse, as he has told me several times."

"Thank you sir for saying that. I like to have a good time as you know, but when a job is on I will try my darnedest to succeed."

"Now let's get on with our own briefing. When you return to England you will be given a week off to find a place to live in Cambridge, and to start your new job working with Burt. You will still keep your office in the embassy and use it anytime you need. I recommend you give Nicola your IDs and embassy keys when you are on an assignment. Your new German passport is waiting for you at her house. Do not keep anything from her. She has been checked out along with her family thoroughly. I would also suggest you say as little as you can to her parents."

"The general has heard from ASA Frankfurt, and you are needed for another extraction around the New Year. General Simpson will tell you all about the plan when the time comes."

"Where is the extraction from, sir?"

"You will be briefed in late December, and that is all I know. The asset or assets are being worked on."

"Give the driver your passport, and he will check you in while we finish our briefing. Most important Wright, the West episode, your name will not be in any report, forget it ever happened. Is there anything you need to say?"

"Sir, could you transfer the Prague jurisdiction to my office. I would like to have control of contacts and disbursement of monies."

"Are you sure of this Wright, your duties in the United Kingdom are your first concern. The driver is motioning for you to hurry, call me next week, goodbye."

Nicola and her parents were waiting for me at Heathrow Airport. It was Saturday morning and the jet lag didn't seem to bother me. When we got to their house and over a cup of tea, they wanted to know how my trip went. Nicola becoming bored with my drab tales of being in classes every day, got up and retrieved a package from the sideboard.

She said, "Go on, and open it."

I noticed the postmark was official and the package had "US Embassy Confidential" stenciled on the large envelope. Two passports fell out, a red one and a green one. The red one I gave to her and the other one I put in my pocket.

Her mother Flo asked for and was given the red passport.

A comment in perfect Cockney was, "Well, I never, a diplomatic passport, what name is inside?"

Nicola wanted to know about the other passport.

I had to say something as the three of them was looking at me.

"I need to explain something to you all for now. First, I will be attending Cambridge University in the fall to start a degree course. My place has been granted and a flat will be available by the end of next week for me to move into."

"That is wonderful news darling, we must have a party and tell every one of our friends now. What is the other passport for?"

"It is something I will need for a job at the end of the year in a foreign country, which is all I can say on that matter. I need to go to my bedsit now and get some sleep, if that is okay?"

Jack said, "Sure, me ol' son, you must be knackered."

Nicola walked with me to my place. I have to tell you some more about the other work I am doing for the embassy. Something only you will know and cannot tell anyone else, not even your parents.

"It sounds mysterious, Billy."

"I will see you for lunch around 1 o'clock this afternoon if that is okay. Why don't you come get me and make sure I am awake by then?"

"Yes darling, I will, so glad you are back after such a long time away."

Over at my bedsit the feeling of lying down was so good, all stretched out. I don't remember staying awake that long.

The next morning Nicola was knocking on my door, waking me from a deep sleep. I got dressed and let her in. We soon left for Harrow High Street to find a place for lunch. Being still groggy, she did most of the talking. At least it was a nice walk without it drizzling for a change.

Chapter 10

Cambridge Op. Center

The next weekend was moving day to my new flat overlooking the university. No one would suspect that this was to be an observation and operation center for spying on future members of the British Civil Service and its intelligentsia services recruiting new people.

Hopefully history will not be repeated by trusting the word of anyone outside of our own secure environment. Are we becoming insular, you can bet your last ruble we are. We are now in their house playing by our rules. It's time to go report for my summer job down on the river.

Burt was waiting for me on the banks of the river Cam. "'ello mate, are you ready to rock and row down the river?"

"I got ya hooked with some posh git for ya to learn da ropes; don't pay him no mind, he's a bit of a whiner. The bloke was on the Cambridge rugby team, and after a couple of days of being trained by him, I found out he was alright. Just because he speaks slow and precise doesn't mean he's a git. We got along famously to a point he invited me to go shooting pheasants on his parents estate.

I would have loved to go, but couldn't risk being found out in case someone in his family spoke fluent German. It was always enjoyable having a few beers together after work most afternoons and discussing the pretty girls we punted. If only there was a way to ask him if he would like to join our team without him thinking I was some kind of crackpot. I needed someone to watch my back at student group parties on weekends.

I didn't want to call him the disrespectful name of the git anymore to Burt, his name was Bartholomew David Chesterfield. I called him David from then on. It wasn't long before I recruited him after he answered my questions with a 90 percent favorable score.

On one late evening after a few beers, he talked of how his parents were making him work odd jobs for spending money with waiting tables in a pub. I asked him why not get another job. He had tried as it was obvious with so many students and very few casual jobs available he was lucky to get any job at all.

After I bought him another beer I asked if he ever went to any anti- American Vietnam War rallies. He said there was a girl he fancied who asked him to join her. Most of the students who were at the protest were not the types he would like to be associated with, especially when they started doing drugs.

The next morning it was starting off slow with the punts, so I asked Burt to give me the rest of the day off day off so I could go to London. I really needed to talk to the general about hiring David. He wanted to go with me, but we couldn't both be off at the same time.

David was getting a measly wage of 10 pounds a week for working 40 hours busing tables. The agency could do better, but what could he do to be a help. Anyway it wouldn't begin until October with the start of the new school year and last to the end of June. Forty pounds a month would be worth every bit to have someone cover my back. He could be checked out by the Embassy security services well in time to be part of my team, before the fall semester began.

General Simpson had agreed to meet with me at noon over lunch, in the embassy cafeteria. I was early with the purpose of visiting my part-time secretary.

She got up from typing to give me a hug and saying at the same time, "Ain't you a sight for sore eyes?"

I needed to know some things before meeting the general.

"Is everything running smoothly, what about the general and his relationship with the ambassador?"

"I shouldn't be telling you this, but what the hang, the general is bored because of the high ups here will not meet with him to go over important stuff. He said they keep him out of some loopy what name."

"What would Tibby do? They want to keep him out of the loop, which is a euphemism used sometimes for explaining a concern or problem."

"Ain't that funny, every time Mrs. T called, she would ask in a Southern drawl iss Tibby ian? That other stuff is foreign to me ducky."

She wasn't rude talking of Mrs. Thibodeau's Southern accent, how could she with her Cockney twang just as different? I enjoyed hearing both accents.

"Yes, it is funny; however, Mr. T. would not want to hear Tibby spoken out in public. When they were young that would have been innocent and cute."

"Yes love, 'ow is it that they talk like that?"

"If only others could see us as we see ourselves. I must go; the general would not be pleased if I am late."

With the time a little before noon, the cafeteria is mostly empty, which was fortuitous. A table was needed as far away from the buffet line as possible, and from anyone who was within earshot of our meeting. Getting him to see my reasons for wanting to hire someone to protect me was going to be a hard sell. The psychological aspect of him needing me around at all costs had to be delivered in a convincing way.

The general walked in and motioned for me to go over and join him in getting some lunch. We exchanged pleasantries as we shuffled along pointing to the food we wanted, so the server could plunk it on our plates. This wasn't the best place to eat or have a serious talk, but if his time was scarce, then it would have to do.

Just as we sat down he asked, "Why did you need to see me?"

"General, I wanted to ask you if there were any funds leftover in the CIA expense account for this year that could be allocated towards my assignment in Cambridge. These funds have to be shielded from the embassy's auditors. For now all that is needed is 120 pounds until the end of December. If my strategy works then another 240 pounds will be needed for the first six months of next year. I would understand if you deem this plan to be unacceptable."

"Okay, Wright, let's hear the plan."

"I need someone to be in my corner at targeted student parties, which would provide me a way into subversive groups and faculties. Someone watching to make sure my drinks are not compromised by serums or drugs. Also this person would be needed to keep an eye on our associations when I am in Eastern Europe at the beginning of next year."

"Is your girlfriend the needed accomplice?"

"No sir, I will need someone with physical strength and knowledge of the university's clubs and where students are housed. Nicola wants nothing to do with any spy game."

"Smart girl, I do not see a problem. You are correct in your summation that a backup is needed just in case you go missing behind the Iron Curtain. Give our secretary the person's name you have in mind; I want to meet him by the beginning of October to give my final approval."

I was relieved that the general was agreeable to my plan. After giving the secretary David's name in a sealed envelope inside another sealed envelope, I left for Cambridge.

Back punting tourists around the next day, David was curious what I had really got up to yesterday. I told him I went to see my fiancé in Harrow and had spent a wonderful afternoon with her.

He said, "Burt acted strange yesterday with me being away. He asked me all kind of questions about you and what you are like. He didn't seem to be himself."

"That is strange David; I don't know what to make of it."

"In psychology class he would be analyzed as somewhat paranoid by needing to know what you were up to. It has nothing to do with him as to what you do on your days off."

"Feel like a beer after work?"

"I have to work in the pub tonight. Come around, I'll supply you with beer all night. That is a way to pay you back for the beers you bought me in the past."

"My girlfriend is coming in tonight, we will have dinner there."

"I wouldn't if you want to impress her, the food is terrible."

We both laughed as we poked fun at each other. Burt seeing this scolded us for not paying attention to a group of tourists wanting to be pushed down the river.

Four weeks from the time I had seen the general, a letter was sent to my flat from the embassy, requesting mine and David's presence the following Monday. I had questioned my friend on his views of different governments in the west for the past month. It was important to see if he had any Marxist or communistic views or leanings towards that philosophy. I was satisfied he was as blue as Winston Churchill.

Today had to be the time to ask him what he thought about working undercover for the CIA with me as his mentor. While working between trips on the river, I asked him to go for a beer after work. I was buying to celebrate my birthday. It was set, now to find a quiet place to talk.

As we were leaving Burt told us that the season was coming to a close, and one of us had to be let go. We were to flip a coin to see which one. He had already let another student go that morning.

David said, "I need the job, do you mind ol' boy if I'm the one that stays?"

"Yes, I will volunteer since I have something to do elsewhere. Now let's go get that cold beer."

Chapter 11

Low-level Op. Center

We found a pub with an empty garden to have our first strategy meeting. I hoped it was going to be a first of many.

This was as awkward a start to a briefing as I ever had. I didn't know how to begin asking him about joining my team.

David asked, "You seem to be a million miles away, is there something troubling you? If you need the job, I will gladly let you work with Burt. I can start cleaning tables at the pub."

"No, it's nothing to do with the punting job. I have a serious question to ask you about another place of employment where you can go to school and keep playing rugby. This job is as nondescript as you will ever find or have to do. It isn't a normal

9 to 5 job and I have talked it over with my boss for the last two months in London," I replied.

"David, you have been checked out by an American security team and I have been asked to recruit you to work for the American Intelligence Services out of London while going to Cambridge."

"You are joking aren't you? You can't be a spy, you're a regular bloke. Your name doesn't fit, that is all. Ludwig is your name, isn't it? I really don't know what to say."

"Look David, ask your father about this if you have to. You will be a low- level operative, a job of covering my back while we are in Cambridge. The work will be more rewarding than washing dishes and the pay isn't great, but it is a sight better than pub wages."

"Hang about you; there were noises about my parents being investigated by the Yanks from Whitehall. Tell me that wasn't your lot asking questions, and why wasn't I asked about it if it's about me?"

"You were David, in a discreet, way so as not to telegraph why the agency wanted to know all of your past."

"If I said yes, what happens next? What about the pay, how much an hour? Is it by the job or what?"

"We have a scheduled meeting with my boss on Monday at 10 a.m. in London. Your pay is 40 pounds a month and with going to university, the hours you work will be a lot less than what you did the last school year busing tables."

"What if I wanted more money, what then?"

"I negotiated the wages for you, that is all we are offering. If that is not enough, you will have to go back to cleaning up after messy students in the pub. We can continue as we are as if you were never approached by me. The only problem is if you decline this job offer you mustn't tell anyone, for my safety will certainly be at risk this winter."

"I will go see my dad this weekend and will let you know Sunday evening. You will have to cover for me by working, if that is agreeable to you, no negotiating."

That broke the tension as we laughed about his demands. Burt knew something was up since David was supposed to be working Saturday and I showed up to cover for him.

Burt grouchily asked, "What's your game, mate? Where's that posh git, he's 'posed to be working? I must be out of me bleedin' mind haven you two workin' 'ere."

"Burt, he had to go see his parents this weekend. It must have been a last-minute decision. I know he is sorry not working today with you, he thinks you are a good bloke."

"That's al'right then innit?"

He was in a better mood now and even agreed to have a beer with me after work.

David arrived at my flat the next evening, and asked for me to go to the pub with him. He wouldn't say anything until he had a pint of dark bitter beer in his hand.

He started with, "You're buying; I will get a table where we can talk."

"Well, what did your dad say?"

"He talked to your boss, the general in the embassy, about the investigations last week. He was not pleased that someone was asking according to him, silly questions around London."

"What did he say?"

"It's a good thing you were in good standing with your boss, which helped a lot. He said it would be alright to try it for a few months to see how everything works out."

"Great news David, I was on pins and needles all weekend, not to mention having to smooth over Burt with you going away without telling him, and that wasn't easy." I bought him a beer and said, "You may be delayed until Tuesday, and I had to take off Monday as well." He was not pleased with me at that moment. I should have waited until he downed his third beer; he was okay with it then."

"Where do you get the money to buy everyone drinks?"

"It's part of my expense account."

"What? All this time you're buying my beer and I was beholding to you or I thought I should be. You could have told me it wasn't your money you were spending."

I started laughing, after a few seconds he found the funny side of what has been going on for the last nine weeks.

"Now, what about your mother? Is she okay with you being interviewed by the Yanks?"

"She doesn't know; father keeps everything quiet and what do you mean interviewed, I thought I was in."

"It may be a formality, but on Monday you will still have to pass the interview. My boss has the last word; I can only recommend you and give my reasons for doing so. Now we need to call it a night and get some rest, 6 a.m. is going to be here before we know it."

After catching the early train we walked into the agency's office 30 minutes early, the secretary got up to welcome the new agent in.

She said, "Billy, introduce me to the young man. By the way, there is some mail on your desk."

David looked puzzled when she called me Billy.

"David, meet my secretary Miss Peabody."

In my office David said, "Billy, is that your name or is there another one you go by? An office in the embassy is beyond comprehension, with a secretary."

"That is my real name."

At that moment David was escorted into the general's office. I was told to go downstairs to get some breakfast.

After an hour I went back upstairs and there was no sign of David. The secretary heard me and came out of Simpson's office, then pointed for me to go back downstairs.

After another hour Miss Peabody came to get me and brought David down to get something to eat. She had to stay with him as he wasn't allowed to walk around inside the building. I was told the general wanted to see me right away.

He said, "Mr. Chesterfield will fit in with the right training that you are going to give him. He may have a future with us; we will have to wait and see how he handles himself. His father and I spoke for a long time concerning why his family was being investigated."

By not telling David anything, even your name, is commendable; you do still surprise me sometimes Wright. We talked about what was expected of him and he will fill you in on everything we discussed. Miss Peabody has two first-class train tickets for you, where you can start his debriefing in a carriage that usually is empty of passengers. I want to see you back here towards the end of November with a progress report. You will be notified of the date and time. Now take off before the commuters start their way back to Cambridge and you won't be able to talk."

We were the only ones in the first class compartment. David was smiling as if he knew he had passed the interview.

"Well," he asked, "What did the general say to you?"

"He thinks you have the makings for being a very good agent with the right training in ways to defend yourself."

"The general wants me to start taking judo as soon as possible. He wants you to train me on how to be aware of my surroundings. He also told me that my job was to see that no one gets close to you to do you harm, like spiking your drink or having several cowards banding together to attack you; whereas one-on-one you would do just fine. He went on to tell me about your assignment in Cambridge."

' "David, we have to plan out the best way of obtaining information from our targets once the fall session starts. You are officially on the payroll starting today. You will be paid through a third party with bank drafts going into your account. Give Burt two weeks' notice and we are now officially working on our next move. No notes are to be taken. In other words, we write nothing down that pertains to the assignment. We will meet after work and then after school during the first semester."

Back at my flat we set our agenda for the next three weeks. He would tell me about the students who were close to their leftist lecturers. There was one older man who looker Russian, or was definitely a foreigner, hanging around outside one of the main lecture halls last year on several occasions.

I asked, "David, do you know anything about the Apostle Club within the university?"

"One of my rugby team members, who is a very bright student, is an Apostle Club member."

"Would you feel uneasy asking him to give you the names of other members?"

"Yes, I would; however, we could go to one of their haunts where they meet once a month. It is at the pub I work for, or used to work for."

"You need to work one night a month or whenever the club meets there to see if they leave any paper or notes lying around. I will stay away so they wouldn't suspect we knew each other off campus."

"The student that Burt told to leave before us is a member."

"I thought he was a loner and maybe lacked confidence around other people. Besides that, he was alright, just a quiet type, not expressive or confrontational."

"Yes, he is alright, except around his mates where he is expressive enough on world views. I will let the publican know I will work when he has a student group reserve a room. That group is the only one who meets there because it is a bit down market. It's a working man's pub, which is why you don't see any birds from school in there. Not many other students like them because they talk about helping the ordinary man, but won't associate with them."

"David, do you remember some of the names attending the meetings last year or ones that have graduated? What about the Cambridge Dons, do they show up at these monthly meetings? What do they talk about when you enter the room?"

"I really have never listened to their conversations or know if they write down anything. Wait, I remember they do tick off names of attendees and minutes of the meeting. Most of the times they are still there after we are closed and I have to keep serving them drink."

Perfect, you could pretend to be asleep outside the door and listen to see what their plans are for the school year."

"The pub will tell me when the meeting room is booked for. No one else will do the work I do, or is trustworthy enough to let the owner go home on late nights."

Chapter 12

The Apostles' Creed

My new recruit David was given the information on the first meeting of the Apostle Club. It was to be the second week of October to induct new members. That meant all of the overseers would be present. That was going to be an opportunity one dreams about in undercover covert actions, having all the pigeons in one small area. We desperately needed a mole inside the club.

October 7 was coming soon and Nicola wanted time to reconsider our plans to be married. She wasn't so sure marrying a person who had chosen a questionable career was conducive to having a normal family life and eventually having children. Dating was a better option, with the odd weekend away by the beach or up in the Cotswold's. That particular week was going to be busy for me and with the impending trip around the New Year, it would not be nice for Nicola hanging around and wondering what I was up to.

Our supposedly wedding date was here and Nicola arrived in Cambridge to spend the weekend. She met David and thought he was a real English gentleman. I told her that she made the right decision to postpone the wedding since I would have to be away most of January starting on New Year's Eve. She was relieved to know that she could stay in Harrow and attend the celebration with friends; however, we would spend Christmas together at her parents' house.

When Nicola left to go back to Harrow, David and I couldn't wait to put into motion our first covert operation. He was the mole masquerading as the publican on the night of the Apostle Club induction party.

The weekend of the meeting was upon us, with David working the October 14th Apostle gathering in the backroom of the pub. I suggested that if he found the group were getting careless and needed another drink to make them even more so, regarding their paperwork, he was to keep the drinks flowing. I told him to have the pub buy the last drink or I would splurge if he thought it would be pay off for us.

On the night of the meeting David woke me up at midnight and asked me to come over to the pub quickly and bring my camera. I wondered what was up as I hurried through the narrow and wet cobblestone streets.

Instead of going straight in, I peered through the back window to see what this summons was all about. Most of them were passed out sleeping in chairs with three bodies on the floor; and there was blood all over the place.

I went back to the front door to find it open and quietly slipped in, closing the door behind me without making a sound.

David said, "The last one passed out when I called you. That foreigner, who was here last year, is on the floor with a knife in his hand."

The photographs had to be taken while David cleaned up the empty beer mugs, and was out of the room so he couldn't be accused of having tampered with the evidence. A prized snapshot was with a hand holding the knife that belonged to the Russian

Volkov, and unfortunately one of the bodies on the floor was Leos. *Unbelievable,* thinking to myself, *what an early Christmas present this was, to find an offensive lecturer in the middle of a crime scene!*

I told David "Get some hot water and plenty of towels so we can clean the blood off of my friend Leos."

When he left the room to get the towels, I went through the Russian's pockets to retrieve his ID and money. He was loaded with enough cash to buy everyone's allegiance at the party. General Thibodeau mentioned that Volkov was known to the American intelligence agencies as a man who would stop at nothing to capture or kill his targets. Somehow he had to be dealt with before he found out about Leos and me, or who we were.

Using the knife, I pierced his jugular vein to finish him off as he was almost dead anyway, and that somehow relieved my conscience. After doing the unthinkable to keep us safe, I then placed the other student on the oozing blood so David couldn't see the expanding puddle of blood when he came back into the room.

It was important then to empty the pockets of the other two young men on the floor. After placing the Russian's money in a student's hand and the Russian driver's license on the floor beside them, I took more incriminating photographs.

After gathering up the planted material, I took the IDs of everyone else since they had all passed out.

I placed all of the other IDs and the Russian's papers in my pockets before David returned to the room; so if he was questioned he couldn't say for sure who did the thieving.

When he got back I said, "Help me with Leos so we can get him to my flat."

"Do you know him?" David asked.

"Yes, now let's hurry and get him out of here. I have to get back before they all wake up."

At the flat we put Leos on the couch with a blanket over him. After David had left to go back to the pub, I started emptying the IDs onto the dining room table. It was important for me to start copying the names and addresses into a workbook.

I hurried back to the pub and stuffed the money and IDs into the Russian's pocket and into the other hand without the knife.

I told David, "Call the police, since there is too much blood on the floor to clean up as well as on some of the members close to the body. Don't worry, the passed out professor at the head of the table will get this episode swept under the carpet. As for the Russian, with his diplomatic immunity, this incident never happened. All of the wounds look superficial, and they all seem to be alright at first glance; only when the police start moving the bodies will they find out that the Russian is dead."

"Now, you demand to be searched by the police because of money being involved. Get all of the names of the policemen from the lowest ranks to the one in charge. The police will hopefully search you back at the police station. The first thing they will do is ask you to leave with a policeman, while the university clean-up team does their work; and you are not a witness to the actual disposing of the incriminating evidence.

"Protecting the university's image will be the most important task by the police higher echelon.

The university heads will say if anyone is hurt or even killed, it is unfortunate. Do not tell them about me taking photographs. I will drop them into the post after they are developed, and I have had time to go through them."

"How can you know that?"

"All of last year, have you heard of anyone charged with a sex crime at the university? Think about it David."

I was back in my flat when sirens could be heard from the vicinity of the pub. Leos was still out cold. I put a bucket and a towel by his head just in case he was sick. Having moved the notes after jotting them down again for a second set, I went to my bedroom and locked the door, just in case Leos woke up feeling lost or confused, and wanted to investigate to see where he was and who was there.

It was good to get a few more hours sleep. I got up to make a cup of coffee as Leos was awakening. He saw me and the look he gave me was like he was seeing a ghost from the past. I laughed and told him to lie there, and just think before asking anything. He needed a cup of coffee to sober up.

It was Sunday morning, the one day I cooked myself a full breakfast. I knew he couldn't handle bacon, sausage and eggs. He had to have dry toast and maybe by lunch he could eat something more substantial. After eating his toast he started coming around, but was still confused as to why I was in a flat in Cambridge of all the places in the world to be.

I talked while he listened, but after all of my explanations he was still confused and literally fell back to sleep. David called and wanted to tell me something. He sounded worried and said he was on his way over. Whatever he needed to tell me was too important to keep to himself.

When he knocked on the door, I got on my coat and took two chairs outside for us to sit on the sidewalk.

I told David, "I need to talk to Leos before he leaves here. I have something to tell him that he only can hear from me."

"You know that bloke?"

"Yes, I do."

"He is a foreign student and you know him? I overheard them praising his communist background before his initiation. How can you know him?"

"Listen David, I helped in getting him out of Czechoslovakia toward the end of last year. He thinks he owes me, I know him to be an upstanding young man. I don't want him to see you here just in case he has turned red."

"You just don't write a letter to a Soviet Bloc country and ask if it is alright if someone can come see you. People are getting killed every day trying to escape."

"I was recruited for a specific job by the agency and that was to get him to the West. Going behind the Iron Curtain was risky and exciting at the same time. It had to be done by someone who had to fit a certain profile as a student. Did they search you at the station?"

"Yes, I had to strip down to my underwear and wait while they went through my pockets. The desk sergeant and the one escorting me back were the only ones in the station. You went into the Soviet territory?"

"Yes, no more for now, did they ask you any questions?"

"No, they said they may want to question me later on. They assumed it was just a drunken ritual."

"Go back and wash the clothes you were wearing in very hot water and put them back on. The police will come and collect your clothing probably today. You must go now and quickly wash them and then leave. I will meet you later on at the cafe in the train station about 4 p.m."

When I got back inside the flat and made a noise putting the chairs down, Leos woke up. He wasn't feeling well and was white as a sheet of paper. After making him another coffee he started to remember the previous night. He wanted to know why I was there in Cambridge. He really wasn't ready for any type of logical conversation, so I told him to take a shower and get some more sleep. I was going to see my girlfriend.

Nicola met me at Waterloo Station where we found a pub to have lunch. After giving her the film to have developed in Harrow, she said she would bring it back to Cambridge the next weekend.

After a few hours window shopping with Nicola, I left on a train that would get me back to see David at the Cambridge Station. I was in the cafe when he came in; he motioned to see if I wanted a cup of tea. Yes, I motioned back. He told me that last night was a bit of a blur, and how he thought it was awful behavior by the professor and his student club members.

I asked, "Did the police interview you again?"

"Yes, you were right. I had to take off my clothes in front of them, even my underwear. They put everything in a bag, along with my dirty rugby gear. This suit I have on is all I have left to wear. I look like someone going to a funeral."

"Were you able to memorize the names of the police from last night and today?"

"The two today were the same ones from last night. There was a high- ranking inspector with the other two this afternoon, who asked if I had seen anything of the fracas. I told him I dropped off to sleep in the lounge and woke up after a little while later to go tell the group I had to close up, so that I could go home. That was when I saw blood on the floor. He told me to forget everything I had seen, like it never happened."

"You were right about them making everything go away. The pub owner came over to tell me they wouldn't let him in to clean up this morning to get ready for the lunch crowd. He was told it was clean and I was the one who cleaned it up before leaving. What about the foreigner in your flat, what is his story?"

"He is still too out of it to be asked any questions. I need to go back and cook him something that he can keep down. Thanks for the names of the police officers. Now go and see the publican and find out if everything was clean. Don't mention you didn't do the cleaning and we will see where that leads us."

"Before I go Billy, the police were asking if anyone left after I discovered the fracas. I told them again I was asleep part of the evening and early morning, and didn't notice anyone leave when I was awake. By the way, they are looking for the bloke in your flat."

Chapter 13

Volkov Got in the Way

When I got back to my flat, Leos was still on the couch and just waking up again. I put some minestrone soup on the stove to heat up for him. He needed some liquids and a little food for him to get back to feeling normal. I noticed he was back to wearing ear rings and a silver stud through his nose. He looked the part of a subversive left wing idiot.

His appearance would be helpful to plant him in the targeted groups without making him suspicious of being a mole. Now to get Leos back on his feet again, and ready to answer a few well thought-out questions; this had to be a friendly interrogation.

He wanted to know how and why I was here at a place he ended up in going to university.

Leos said, "Billy, I am so, so sad you found me like this. They made me drink until I passed out as part of my way into their club. Those people were awful the way they acted, especially the two professors who were in charge of our getting to know each other."

"Leos, you are young and will do foolish things. I was like that once, now hopefully those days are over for me. You said there were two professors there when the meeting started."

"Yes, they both introduced themselves to the new members and gave short, funny speeches."

"Do you remember their names?"

"Yes, why do you need them?"

"I am attending the university as you are, and would like to know who my lecturers are."

"That is wonderful news Billy; we can hang around together and party with new friends."

"My name is Ludwig here and I am from West Germany, please call me Ludwig when someone else is around."

"I don't understand, what are you saying?"

"My being here is for gathering information on certain individuals."

"Alright Billy, I need to help you since you have helped me and my mother and father. The Apostle group isn't something I would want to be associated with."

"You will need to part of that group for now to help me observe the two professors and all of its members. Never write anything down for fear of someone finding your notes. Act shy and reserved at all times, so you will be considered a follower. So most likely you will not be asked to carry out unseemly tasks on your own."

"Now think Leos, this is most critical. The Russian at the party, did you speak to him at any time?"

"I can't remember, I think so, I probably spoke to everyone before we started drinking. How do you know who was there?"

"The Russian is one of the people I had to watch. Ask the other students at the party if you behaved like you should. Do not ask the professors, they are too cunning. The police want to ask you some questions;

they are not like the police in Czechoslovakia. They will be nice to you and take your word as truthful as long as you say you do not remember anything."

"I will do as you say Billy, sorry Ludwig. Do you know how I was able to get a place at Cambridge University?"

"Most likely you received a grant or funding with help from the American government."

"After this school year, will you think about becoming an agent, so you can help others escape to the West?"

"That is not for me. I would be afraid if by chance the secret police were going to catch me. Your country has helped my family more than we could ever repay you; it is cowardly of me to decline helping you by going into any Soviet territory. Is there any other way I can help you in your work?"

"Maybe there is, let's plan to meet once a week at the train station cafe when you have a half day off from school, not here again. I think it is best for now if we are not seen as knowing each other."

"That is good; will every Wednesday afternoon at 2 p.m. be alright for you Ludwig?"

"Yes, see you then. It is dark now so you must go; no one must see you coming out of my place, especially the police."

Leos, now working as my mole was great news. I would need to go see the general as soon as possible.

There was a knock at the door.

"Who is it?"

"David, let me in. I thought the foreigner would never leave. I went to the pub to get my pay."

"How much of a bonus did you get?"

"You are one scary bloke Yank; you must have the place bugged, there is no way you could have known about my big tip."

"Hush money, the owner would have received four times what you were paid to keep quiet. That was cheaper than what it would have cost to save the university's reputation by placing adverts in all of the national newspapers. Did he say anything else?"

"One of the pub's customers saw a body bag carried out and placed into an ambulance. Did you know someone was dead when you took the photos?"

"No, the Russian seemed hurt but not dead. The hole is getting deeper as they keep digging to bury their dirty little secrets. I will be away on Tuesday having a meeting with the general. You need to keep an eye open by working at the pub tomorrow night. Just don't tell the general about the pub job when you see him again; he can't assume you are moon lighting away from the agency."

"What about the foreigner?"

"He's kosher. It's time for you to leave now. I have to get some much- needed sleep."

I called Andrea to let her know she was on my mind, and that I wished to see her again in the forest. She knew that was code for another rendezvous in the Bohemian Forest, probably around the New Year. It had to be a quick call so the phone tap would be somewhat vague of information.

Going to sleep was blissful and quick. As soon as I woke up, it was time to put together the paperwork for the general, and to tell him that it was most important he see me tomorrow morning.

When I called Miss Peabody, the secretary hinted someone else was in the office and so she couldn't talk.

I asked, "Perhaps he could call me back this morning?"

"The weather is supposed to be better this afternoon, love. I will see you then, be on time."

Someone was coaching her in how to use coded messages, and I was impressed by Miss Peabody's newfound skills. I then had time to go to the university's bookstore for supplies. As I walked there, I thought what a wonderful place to be in school. The library was stuffy with smoke and dust flying through the air, but it was a good place to read all of the top London newspapers.

For over an hour I perused the tabloids and saw no mention of any deaths in the center of Cambridge or for that matter in a pub. I knew for sure the fix was well cemented and set. It was time to implement a plan for the big sting and have the dons' play by my rules now.

Back at home I was ready to use my university workbook to map out the clandestine operation. Masking my strategy as a practice for Latin should confuse anyone outside of the lecturers.

The general called to say he was available the next morning as he had to be in Edinburgh for a meeting at the American Consulate there. I suggested we meet at Kings Cross Station in the morning before he boarded his train.

He said, "We will meet on the train for breakfast. Be there to catch the 9 a.m. train to Edinburgh. Meet me in the first-class compartment. Miss Peabody will see you there with your ticket. Goodbye."

Either paranoia was rampant or he knew his phone was bugged. I wished I could have told him I had an appointment at 2 o'clock tomorrow afternoon.

The rest of the day was spent studying classic Latin, mixed in with a little southern pig Latin; also, I slipped Leos a note to let him know that we would meet at 5 instead of 2 the next day.

The next morning, I met Miss Peabody as planned; and after a welcomed kiss on the cheek, she gave me the round trip tickets.

She whispered, "A MI5 officer was standing in front of me when you called yesterday, asking if we had anyone working in Cambridge. Now you better hurry and board the train."

The general was waiting and was already sipping a cup of tea.

"Well Wright, you have until the third stop to brief me, which will be Doncaster where you will have to turn around and go back. That will give you exactly one and a half hours to tell me everything you have."

"Yes sir, first of all, Volkov was killed the other night in Cambridge in a suspicious manner."

"Wright, stop! Did you have anything to do with that murder or were you in close proximity to the scene of the murder? I had to lie to the British Intelligence services about not having someone in Cambridge. That was the first time I had lied to the man as he has been a close confidant in the past."

I couldn't answer him, and he wouldn't want me to if I was the one responsible.

I continued, "A former asset named Leos, who you are familiar with, is enrolled in Cambridge. He was part of the group where the fracas involving Volkov was. A party got out-of-hand when several of the group were cut with a dagger, which probably belonged to Volkov. Our new agent David was working at the pub, undercover. The two of us got Leos to my flat before David was told to call the police. The IDs and other papers from all of the party attendees were copied down in the flat, before I returned to the pub to put everything back."

"You seemed to be targeting that particular group, why and what is the name of the fraternity?"

"They are called the Apostles."

The general rudely interrupted me before I could tell him why, then he was quiet for at least five minutes; it seemed he was running this information through a thought processor. It was awkward waiting for him to continue.

He looked really concerned as he said, "We will have to move you out of Cambridge to a safe place."

"You must not, sir. I have everything under control and it is working out better than planned.

Please hear me out before you make this call. The university has cleaned up the scene, and they have swept it under the carpet. They are co-conspirators with the police chief and only God knows who else. There was nothing in any newspapers throughout the United Kingdom the following day. I read every newspaper printed in London thoroughly over the past 48 hours.

"Sir, this is part of the same group or club whose past members caused so much damage in the 1950s and '60s by selling secrets to the Soviets. I have someone planted in the group, and he is as loyal to me as I am to you."

"Wright, if the authorities find out you have had anything to do with the Volkov murder, you will have no one to back you up. I will have to deny that you are one of our men."

"Sir, I still have an ace up my sleeve to play if needed."

"They are bringing our breakfast. Let's eat while I think this out Wright."

When we had finished there was about 20 minutes to go before we got to the stopping off point.

"Okay, Wright, you play it out as you see fit. I am glad Volkov is out of the picture. I am not sure the ambassador is as pleased as I am. He was in a bad mood yesterday as he showed his rear end when I had to lock my heels in front of his desk. I need you to find out if the dead Russian was a double or if he was a straight Russian agent. Can you do this or do you need someone from the field to come in?"

"Give me a couple of months to shake a few branches; don't move on it until I tell you I can't do it."

"Okay Wright, we will meet again when you are ready. You had better stay away from the embassy for a while."

"One last thing, sir. When you hear about another agent taking Volkov's place, I need to know where and what flight he is on. He may want to snoop around the crime scene or get in touch with the big fish at the university. I need to know what he looks like. This is my stop or shall I carry on to the next stop, which is Newcastle?"

"Stay on lieutenant, if you need to carry on with the conversation."

"I need to keep talking so you will know what to report to Thibodeau as soon as possible, or do you want me to call him?"

For the next hour he listened as I explained what was hopefully going to happen in and around the university. The flat was serving its purpose as a great place to operate out of, well worth the money to keep it rented by the agency, besides it being a very nice place to live. Newcastle was announced as the next stop, and after getting my orders to keep in touch, I was off and running. Before leaving, I was instructed to call Thibodeau myself as the phones in the general's office were most likely compromised.

Chapter 14

The Apostles' Sting

An intercity train traveling back towards London was stopping on the opposite platform. Using logic and taking a chance, since it was heading in the right direction, I got in. From the carriage I noticed the general watching me as I turned around to see his train slowly pulling away; he smiled and waved.

On the way back to Cambridge I thought about the general wanting me somehow to unravel the relationship between Volkov and the ambassador. The answer was most likely in the papers that were in the dead man's jacket. Help was needed for someone to interpret the papers without having anyone locally or in the embassy involved.

Maybe Thibodeau back in the States would know of someone in Langley who was fluent in Russian, and could help me to get to the bottom of this conundrum. I thought of discreetly sending them in a Christmas package addressed to Mrs. Thibodeau.

When I arrived back at Cambridge Station a few minutes before 5, Leos was waiting inside the cafe. He was glad I made it as he acknowledged while he bought a cup of tea.

He said, "You got off a train, were you away last night?"

"Yes, I had to see someone in London. Do you have any more news from the other night?"

"Yes Ludwig, plenty of things to tell you. One of the students at the initiation told me I did not act stupidly or was out of order. The Russian did do a bad thing with his knife. He was drunk and got into an argument with the professor on why Russia will destroy Britain soon. His hate showed how he was using us to destroy ourselves. The professor was infuriated at being made a fool of by someone who wasn't even a college graduate. The Russian pulled out his knife and cut him bad enough to go to the hospital."

"It is becoming clearer now Leos. That is why there was only one professor at the party when the police showed up. Did he come back to the party to confront his attacker later on?"

"No one knows for sure as everyone was passed out by then. The waiter should know; however, he told the police he was asleep. Yes, maybe he could have come back and killed his attacker while he was passed out on the floor. How do you know what the waiter said to the police? Our two professors gathered up everyone who was at the party to go over the police report with them, and work out what to do and say if this gets out. The police let the professors know what everyone had said.

"In the meeting we were told to suspect the waiter of robbing everyone and killing the Russian as he lay on the floor. One professor did all of the scheming; the other professor who was the one who went to the hospital, sat nervously quiet by looking down or away during the whole meeting."

"What are the names of the two professors, and what subjects do they teach?"

"Mr. Winters, the quiet one, is head of mathematics. Mr. Harris, the schemer, teaches literature."

"That is most helpful agent Leos; this is our first clandestine meeting on getting the Cambridge papers or at least the embryonic stages of your first assignment."

We both saw the funny side of us working together; Leos, with all of his body piercing, and me being a foreigner. The lady behind the counter also smiled in agreement, even though she had no idea what we found so amusing.

Leos went on say on a more serious tone, "I am willing to help, like you have helped me in the past. My mother and father talk about you all the time, and they say they are blessed with you as an ally. They have two friends that work in the same laboratory as them in Leipzig, who now want to also defect. Can you help them also?"

"I may be able to. The general has mentioned it once in a meeting. Please ask your parents not to say anything to their friends, except to ask them what day in the New Year they could go outside of the compound to shop. We will talk about this in December; we have work here that has to be done first."

"I understand Ludwig. What can I do to help?"

"Next time we meet it will have to be somewhere more discreet than here. The waitress here will not forget us; she can now associate our meeting with having a joke or a good time. Please keep an eye on your Apostle fellows and the two lecturers. Let's meet up Saturday on the 8 a.m. train to London. I will have your ticket and will be in the first-class section if you don't see me on the platform; until then, Leos we will not communicate."

I had to go the university to get my schedule before they closed. The first priority was to buy a gift and post the letters to Washington. There was so much to do in two hours before the shops closed.

Luckily, I was just in time to get in the door of the admittance office. My schedule was ready and the first class was in two weeks time. I paid the first semester fees as a foreign student, and couldn't wait to get back to my flat to see who my lecturers were. But before reading the schedule, I decided to relax after such a long day. Putting the kettle on and brewing a pot of tea to have in a hot bath was pure luxury to me.

Both professors were on my list of lecturers; it was going to be interesting. Nicola called to see if I could come to Harrow for a party on Saturday night. She would me meet me at Harrow on the Hill Station around noon. That would give us the opportunity to pick up the film, and then get a pub lunch somewhere on High Street.

David came over the next morning with information from the pub's clientele, which included the scheming professor. An envelope from the bank was handed to the owner. We both suspected that the professor was being blackmailed, and must have thought the crime still had a possibility of being leaked. I suggested that David quit now before he was associated with another mishap. He mentioned he had already given his notice in, saying that with school, judo and rugby practice, he was too busy.

We had conjured up a plan to disrupt the Apostle Club's agenda of indoctrinating new communist recruits by encouraging students not to join the academic elite club, but to start a new association.

David wanted to know, "Are you going to Trinity College."

"No St. Johns, why?"

"Prince Charles is going there and everyone will be thoroughly investigated. The rest of the student body will also be checked out, but not as much."

"Great that is all I need."

"He isn't part of any group, so we can safely say our paths will probably never cross. He will be shielded from all of the anti-capitalist troublemakers and other subversive groups."

"We will get together on Tuesday when I get back from London. Keep an eye open for any Apostle activity."

When David left I called the general to see if he had time to meet me on Monday morning at Kings Cross Station.

The general was going to be taking his wife to Brighton for the weekend He suggested Nicola and I join them at the Grand Hotel; he said he would book us a room for Saturday and Sunday night. I asked him to book it for Sunday night only. If she didn't want to go, then at least I could have a meeting with him there.

I called Nicola back and she would love to go to Brighton on Sunday. That was great news saying, "I will see you Saturday."

Saturday came and Leos found me on the train to London. We talked all the way until we got out at Saint Pancras Station, and we walked across the street to Kings Cross Station to get a cup of coffee.

I asked him, "When and where is the next meeting with your club?"

"We always meet on the first Wednesday of each month at the same pub. It is strange we are going back there."

"Thanks Leos, let's meet again next Saturday at 10 a.m. on the train to Ely. We will talk then and have lunch at a great pub on the river called 'The Ship's Inn' after we tour the Cathedral."

"I have to go to Harrow. Nicola will be waiting on the platform for my train to arrive."

It was so good to see her again. We went to get the photographs and then to a nice old world pub. She told me all about the party and who was going to be there, as I perused the pictures.

She asked, "Darling, did you hear anything I said?"

"Yes, Nicola, it will good to see everyone again."

The next morning Nicola's parents drove us to Brighton as they hadn't been there since the war and wanted to go. What could I say?I It was nice of them to offer, even though I wanted only the two of us to travel together.

When we got to the hotel, the general was waiting in the large Victorian, opulent dining room. He invited us all to join them for lunch. Nicola's dad got along with the general and he with him. Her mother and the general's wife also enjoyed each other's company. We excused ourselves to walk on the beach as I went to pay the waiter, but he said it had already been arranged.

When we got back to the hotel the four of them were still talking, by then they were into afternoon aperitifs. We went to check our room as they were happy to talk about the war and how things used to be.

Nicola's parents finally left, and we went out to explore the tiny streets and antique shops.

The next morning, after breakfast, the general and I were left alone to get on with the meeting. He looked through the photographs several times. I remembered the bodies were moved in different snapshots. I can't believe I didn't weed them out. He separated the ones incriminating me or David and stuffed them into his pocket.

Staring at me he said, "You were careless lieutenant. What if someone noticed the bodies were tampered with? No wonder you didn't answer me the other week when I asked if you had anything to do with the Volkov murder. What are you going to do with the other photographs?"

"Sir, I will use them as bait and leverage when needed. Another piece of the puzzle you have to know about is that Volkov had a few papers on him, with one of them having the name of Leos Novak on it. I sent the papers to Thibodeau to have them translated in Langley."

"Why did you do that? We have interpreters in the embassy you could have used; it would be a lot quicker."

"Well sir, are they loyal to you or to the ambassador?"

"I see, two heads are better than one is a true euphemism, isn't it?"

"When you speak to Mr. Thibodeau tell him the papers are in a Christmas gift addressed to Mrs. Thibodeau. One last thing before the ladies come down, Leos asked about the two scientists wanting to defect from East Germany, can we help them as they are valued scientists."

"The plans are being worked on; tell Leos we will need photographs of them in case the couple is switched by the Stasi. I will let you know when your team is ready to have you go join them. Will Leos go with you?"

"No, Leos will work for me here in Britain; he has told me he would not be able to go back to the Soviet Bloc in fear of the authorities apprehending him. Have you heard of when Volkov's replacement will be arriving?"

"No, you may only get a few hours notice to observe him."

"That will be okay, I can be at the airport in three hours if I have to be. When you speak to your replacement in Frankfurt, ask them to have my car serviced and ready to go from now until the end of the year. The keys are in the glove compartment."

"Wright, the ladies are waiting to leave. Call me when we need to meet again. Thank you for coming here. I need to talk to your fiancé before we go."

He approached her and said, "Nicola, tell you parents we did enjoy their company. We will have to get together again soon. Take off Wright, I will settle up."

We hurried out to catch the next train. I wanted to have Nicola all to myself and not have company on the way to London.

After Nicola and I said goodbye at Kings Cross Station, I walked over to catch my train back to Cambridge. Nicola kept the negatives of the incriminating photographs and would keep them at her house if I needed them.

Back at my flat there was a note from David asking me to meet him at 2 p.m. down by the river. I had just enough time to get there. He was talking to Burt when I arrived, with Burt wanting to know what we were cooking up.

I told him, "We usually talk about how we love working with you Burt and how generous you are with your wages."

"Gere away wit you, you do carry on."

When we were alone I asked, "What is it David, why did you want to see me?"

"The publican said the police were around again and wanted to have me help with their investigation of the knife fight."

"David, they are looking for someone to pin the murder on. You have to tell them that Professor Winters left the party after being stabbed by the Russian. He was taken by ambulance to get treatment at the hospital and could have come back while you were asleep. I guarantee you they will close the book and say you are free to go. Remember, the police are guilty of collusion along with the school. After you say all of that, keep quiet and stare at them like you know they want to stitch you up."

The next morning David came by to tell me that the grilling at the police station went as I said it would. Once they heard the name of Winter, they closed up the interview.

We can now set up our sting operation and put it into phase one - the need to get all names of past and present Apostle members from the two professors' files.

The rest of the week was spent getting familiar with where my classrooms were. They were scattered all over that part of town. Attending professor Winters' and Harris' lectures was interesting. I was able to see how they reacted to new students. They seemed to have little tolerance for anyone wanting to get to know them. The one student who was at the party in the pub was in both of my classes with the two offending professors; he was given more time to speak than any other student. I knew why he was favored, whereas the rest of the class had no idea of their secret association.

It was Saturday morning and I had to meet Leos in an hour. As I was getting dressed the phone rang. It was the general telling me the new Russian agent had just boarded the plane for Heathrow. His name was Vladimir Oka, and would be here in four hours at terminal one on Aeroflot 522. Kenny would be waiting outside the arrivals hall to take me back to Kings Cross. He quickly told me that I had better get a move on if I wanted to see Oka arrive, and abruptly hung up the phone.

After hurriedly walking to the train station, I bought two round-trip tickets and waited for Leos. If he wasn't on time I would have to leave without him. It was lucky he was five minutes early. I called out for him to hurry; the train was almost ready to leave.

We boarded and he looked around to say, "We are on the wrong train, Ludwig, no?"

"No, we are on the right train since we are now going to London's Heathrow to see a Russian get off the plane. We have an hour before we change to the underground. We won't be able to talk on the tube since there are too many people, and with the train noise we would have to shout to be heard. Do you have any new information?"

"No, not really. The club members are always telling me things as a way to influence me to hate the Western nations and love the Soviet nations. I keep quiet; they have never lived in a totalitarian country and they are telling me it is better than here. They are lunatics."

"Leos, we have to map out a plan to get the information needed, it is a little dangerous. I need the names of past and present members of the Apostle Club. Can you help me in getting all of the names?"

"Yes, they are in Professor Harris's office sitting on his bookcase. He has shown me some famous names that were members in the past."

"Great, do you think you can copy them for me?"

"Yes, it may take several attempts. Why are you seeing a Russian at the airport?"

"We will see him and hopefully he won't see us. He is the new agent taking over for Volkov, and will be trying to get to the bottom of who killed him. I need to identify him for future observations, and to be able to know his whereabouts and who he associates with.

"When we get to the arrivals hall, I will have the Russian paged and see which one he is. He is arriving on the Aeroflot flight from Moscow. Since most Russian men have the profile of a KGB agent, we need to make sure we pick the right one. I will also try to read the placards for his name as a back-up plan."

Chapter 15

A New KGB Agent

We arrived at the airport and went to the observation deck overlooking the arrivals' ramp. When the passengers deplaned, we tried to pick out the most conspicuous one who could be our spy. A Russian on the observation deck looked more like a spy than any of the other passengers. I looked at him to see if he would telegraph a signal to whoever he was waiting for. He moved his right hand a little and I quickly cast my eyes back at the passengers to see a large overweight man signal back. I then waved at a female passenger who was waving at the observers, hoping the Russian up here would think I was waiting to her.

Once the plane was empty, we went back downstairs to watch for the arrivals to come through. I whispered to Leos that I seen the new agent, and he was going to be picked up by the one on the outside deck. He seemed to concur that my opinion was the correct summation. I wanted to tail them and see where they were going. His driver had probably gone to the restroom.

I told Leos, "There is a driver outside waiting for us. Let me point him out as I don't want the new agent to see you. The Russian may remember you when he goes to Cambridge to meet his new comrades and start his own investigations into the murder of Volkov. Go say hello to Kenny and tell him we will be following a Russian back to London."

I pointed, so Leos could see him, and said, "There he is in the black taxi across the street. The only one without its for hire sign illuminated. He sees me now and is waving."

The Russian was the right one, as the driver was holding a small square cardboard sign that read, "Oka." While he waited for his luggage, I went to get into Kenny's cab.

Kenny's greeting was, "'Ello Guv, the general up in the embassy told me to get down 'ere as fast as I could, wots up?"

"There are two Russians coming out soon and I hope they will need a taxi."

We waited and waited, and when they came out Kenny asked, "Is that them Guv?"

"What made you think they were the Russian?"

"Those two blokes barnet fair (hair) looks like they were cut by a 'edge trimmer and Russians always need a shave. They are getting in one of me mate's taxis."

We followed the taxi towards London. Kenny was keeping his distance so as not to alarm the Russians. There were plenty of black taxis going in both directions; we blended in well.

"I reckon they are headed where your other red was staying. It must be a bleeding commie nest. 'Ere we are Guv, where we been before."

"Can I buy you lunch?"

"Not today, Guv, the missus needs the motor and 'er driver, me."

"Next time Kenny, drop us off at St. Pancras."

"Right Guv. I took a fare from the posh git in the compound (ambassador from the embassy) to meet the other geezer that lived 'ere, 'aven't seen him around lately Guv."

"There is a rumor he was done in."

"It wasn't by chance in the middle of mutton country where you may be staying?"

"Rumor is Kenny, it was close-by."

"These two we followed today Guv, are they 'eaded down the same frog and toad (road)?"

"Can you keep a couple of peepers on them?"

"When will I see you next to give me report to ya your mate doesn't blather much, we're 'ere Guv."

"Thank you Kenny; he doesn't understand Cockney. I will call you in a couple of weeks when I come to see the general."

On the train we settled down for an hour. Leos wanted to know what kind of language the taxi driver was talking. I assured him it was English with a strange dialect. He was also curious why I did not pay him for all of the time he spent with us and for the ride to London.

"Leos, the driver is on a wage from us when he is not busy, I can't say anything more for now."

Back in Cambridge, we were both tired from the long day and went to our own homes. Leos would get the list needed that week and my job there would be completed. The general was working on plans along with the ASA in West Germany for the extraction of a top nuclear scientist and his wife pretty soon. A briefing would be done in Bavaria during the last week of December.

I was back in Professor Harris' classroom when he asked for any students who wanted to go on an exchange course in a foreign country after the Christmas break. Volunteers were being asked for, since foreign students and lecturers were already picked to come to Cambridge.

We were told to peruse the list on the notice board in the students' break room. Grades were not going to be a factor as we were still in the first semester. It was a part of the year's curriculum to broaden one's horizon on different cultures. Harris and Winters were two of the local professors slated to be included in the exchange. Professor Winters was to go to Leipzig and Harris to Prague.

After classes were over, Leos saw me studying the exchange list of universities. He slipped a note in my back pocket.

Back in my flat I read the note. He wanted to meet me at the train station cafe in an hour. I met Leos at the prescribed time and he handed me a number of papers, which were copies of the list I had asked for.

Over coffee he briefed me on other news, "We are having a meeting this Saturday at the pub to meet a new comrade. It may be the Russian from the airport. The papers were copied when Mr. Harris was in his first lecture. There are over 300 names in total. I see you were looking over the list of places we could go; I want to go to America to see my mother and father. Will you help me in choosing a university close to New Mexico where they are? You may not want to go to Leipzig if Professor Winters is going there. He would keep an eye on you."

"The University of New Mexico is the closest place to where your parents are working. No stateside universities were offered. Yes, I will put in for Leipzig or Prague. I probably will not see them when I am at either university because of their dislike for me. Thank you for your help with getting the names, I would safely say the meeting will be with the same Russian. He will ask about the killing; be ready for being suspected of knowing something. They will most likely question each member separately and will watch the reactions of those questioned.

"Let's meet again this Sunday here in the cafe at 4 p.m. Watch what you drink and do not drink anything the Russian gets for you. Have a fisherman's friend lozenge in your mouth so a drink will not taste good."

The next day I put in my request to go to Leipzig as the exchange student, and Prague as my second choice.

Three days later there was still no news of who was going to what university; it was frustrating. The important thing then was to get back to other issues like what to do about the Russian coming to Cambridge to meet his communist brothers.

David and I were waiting on Saturday morning at the station for the 10 a.m. train to see if the Russian was on it.

We came back to the station each hour to watch all trains from London empty out. David had to leave if they were not on the 5 p.m. train. He was working undercover at the Apostle party in the pub, when they needed extra help. The two men we followed from Heathrow were the same ones who got off the train. We followed them to a small hotel by the pub. David went off to the pub, and I went in to overhear the room number being used by the two communists.

I set up a surveillance post outside the hotel. When they left I went inside to ask the clerk if it was alright to wait for a friend who was meeting me there. After an hour he left to go outside for some fresh air. I took the key to the Russian's room from the pigeon hole and replaced it with one that had two keys in it. I sat back down and when the clerk came back inside I left. My plan was to go back to the flat and change into a suit with a trench coat to hopefully fool the clerk. I waited an hour before going back to the hotel and found the outside door locked. The room key was the way into unlock the deadbolt.

After locking the front door behind me with two sliding bolts, I took the stairs to the next floor and went inside the room after knocking on the door. My first thought was to open a window in case I had to jump out into the alley.

After finding and taking two passports and other documents, plus a key that was most likely to their place in London, I hurried out and down the stairs. I put the key back in the right pigeon hole after taking the fake key out.

My aim now was to hurry and catch the next train to London to go through the Russian's flat. There was no way for them to catch a later train now until 4 a.m., which would be the mail train that stopped at every large and small station on the way to London. It was midnight by the time I got to the Russian's flat. Their key worked like a charm, getting me into the building and their flat.

Thankfully, no one else was staying in the two bedroom apartment. It would take all night and morning to go through everything. There was a treasure trove of paperwork and two stacks of cash, which I took along with two pistols, ammunition, a sword cane and what looked like knockout drops that I emptied into two large bottles of vodka.

They would be out cold for a long time, and probably have to be taken to a hospital to have their stomachs pumped out. I put the key on the kitchen counter before leaving. The 7 a.m. train was waiting at the platform as I got to the station. When I got to Cambridge, it was time to go home and get some sleep.

There was a knock on the door by David, which awakened me.

When I opened the door he asked, "You look like you have been up all night. I have to tell you about the party at the pub. There was a lot of shouting by the foreigners at the Apostle members after a few hours of drinking. The Russians left and came back instantly to say someone had broken into their room while they were at the meeting. Where were you last night when all of this was going on?"

"David, the foreigners will be really upset when they get back to their place in London."

"You didn't?"

I shrugged my shoulders and told him, "I can't imagine what you could be thinking, David."

"You are one scary bloke. Back to the reason for me coming here, and I will leave and let you get some sleep. Nothing was admitted by the club members last night. The dons made sure everyone had one of them present when a student was questioned. The Russians were not happy. They said they would never come back to Cambridge again."

There was no chance of going back to sleep knowing I had to stash the stuff from last night's burglary and then meet Leos that afternoon. The Russian documents and copies of the notes Leos took the other day were put into another gift box for Thibodeau. The cash was put into another gift box to be mailed to Harrow for me to pick up the next time I was there. I still had a few gift boxes left to use later, if needed.

Leos was waiting at the station cafe. He seemed relieved to see me walk in. I noticed he had nothing to drink so I ordered two cups of coffee and a couple of scones. He started eating the scone right away so I gave him mine to eat; he was happy to accept the food.

I asked, "Do you not have any money for food?"

"No Ludwig, I need to get a job. Everything here cost more than it did in Czechoslovakia and America."

"You must tell me when you do not have money to eat. I will try to get you an allowance from the general for helping us out here in the United Kingdom."

"Ludwig, I need to work for the general and when you go to Prague, I will go with you and help."

"No, I can't afford to have you get nervous over there and spill the beans, if we are caught, I would have to protect both of us. My first priority will be for me to stay alive and free from the secret police."

"I understand, and yes, my nervousness would show through if anyone threatens to do me damage Ludwig."

"Now tell me, what did the Russians say and do at the meeting, and how were the professors during the inquisition?"

"The two Russians are terrible violent people. Why the students still want to be communist is mind-boggling. They threatened us all if no one admitted to killing brother Volkov. It was so intimidating Professor Winters and Professor Harris said they would tell everyone to go home. We were asked if there were any Americans in our classes. They all of a sudden started to buy us drinks and slapped us all on the back as if they were never rude; they were so fake.

"They were told that the police filed a report and determined it was through a drunken brawl and an accident the Russian agent bled to death. They did not believe such a thing could be the real reason. The Russians left and were back quickly saying someone broke into their room. This made them even unhappier to be in Cambridge."

"Was anything discussed about members going to a foreign country on an exchange program? Did the two professors want a student member to go with them to Prague and Leipzig?"

"Yes, I mean no, they asked some to go and none of them wanted to go in the winter. I was the last one they asked; it looked as if they only wanted British students."

"I put in my request to go Leos, so I could work on getting your parents' co-workers out and the student exchange would be just the cover I need. I still want a photograph of the two wanting to defect."

"Ludwig, I sent a letter asking for the photographs. They will be here before December."

"Can you remember seeing professor Winters or Harris's passports in their offices? I will need to have them, especially if they are about the same build as your parents' friends. Wait until you have the photographs and see which professor could have his identity assumed by one of the defectors, then if it could work. I would take the passport to be doctored."

"That will be risky, but I will have to do it. When will you know if the general is fine with my pay?"

"I will guarantee 10 pounds a week, will that be okay? You will need a bank account, and the money will be deposited in your account at the first of each month."

"That is good news Billy, I mean Ludwig. I can now eat. I have to go and wash clothes before going to school tomorrow."

"Okay Leos, I will see you at school somewhere; remember, you do not know me. The professors must never know of our working arrangement. I know my mantra is always the same to a point of being a nuisance. These perverse teachers of our future leaders need no excuse to get rid of anyone who seems to be getting close to uncovering their warped agenda."

When we finished, I went back to my place to study for tomorrow's first class. I thought about how to approach my lecturer in the morning, to see if he would commit to giving me the Leipzig place.

The next morning after the class was dismissed, I asked Winters if he had decided which student was going to go with him. He stared at me for a few seconds and sarcastically stated it wasn't going to be me, even if he had to leave the invitation unfulfilled. That really did get to me. I left to go to the flat and pick up an incriminating photograph of him at the party, as a way of helping him to change his mind. When I arrived back at the university his room was empty, and so I placed the picture in his desk drawer.

The next morning he was acting very nervously, just as if someone knew of his dark secrets.

His opening words were, "I have made the decision on who I am taking to Prague with me. It will be Ludwig as he is the top student; this will be a lesson to all of you who could be as attentive as he is. Will you see me after class Ludwig?"

This was getting interesting, I wondered what he would say, the pompous ass.

Chapter 16

The Sting Hurts

When class was over and we were alone, Professor Winters fumbled nervously in his top desk drawer to find the incriminating photograph.

He shouted, "Do you know anything about this photograph left in my desk? I know it was you Ludwig; it is something a Nazi would do, using blackmail for their evil purpose. You are a German, are you not?"

The picture was thrown at me; I let it go past without trying to catch it. After bending down to pick up the evidence I had to say something even if it sounded dumb.

"This is a disturbing piece of photography, sir. Is that you lying on the floor? Were you inebriated? It must have been a wild party, sir. I have no idea who or what you are talking about. Why on earth would you say I was responsible? You must contact the police if you are being taken advantage of sir."

"The police were contacted and they are going through your room. They should be finished by now. What do you have to say to that Von Wilhelm?"

"Do they work for you or the university, sir? Or is there a darker side to this problem? I really think this is an inappropriate practice you have ordered. I did have a lot of money in my room for living expenses and money to get me back to Germany. If any of the money is missing, I will have to file a report to have it returned. I have 5,000 pounds in cash, and another 2,000 marks that will have to be accounted for.

"Oh yes, because of my wealth, a video is ongoing showing activity by possible intruders. Please let the police know I would like the cash back in my possession by 5 p.m. Now tell them I will not permit police procedural delays, like filling out a report. Can I count on you sir to help me, since they seem to be working alongside you and the university administrators?"

"You will not get away with blackmailing me or the police or the university, I want the remainder of the photographs and all of the negatives; now get out before I throw you out myself."

On the way out of the university, I stopped at the chapel and asked the vicar if he could go with me to see who was in my house. He wasn't doing anything at that moment so he agreed, especially since I seemed to be in a state of bother; and I had placed a 20 pound note into the collection box.

We left immediately for my flat. Police were still there. They were embarrassed when I opened the door with the university vicar by my side.

I acted surprised saying, "Oh my, what are you looking for? Maybe I can help you find whatever it is."

The sergeant said, "We have a report you are in possession of offending pornographic material."

I turned around and asked the vicar, "Maybe we should leave and go see the chief inspector and look at the report he says they have."

As we went to leave the sergeant said, "The report is confidential and you will not be permitted to read it."

"I understand officer; we will go see the station chief and he can ask me any questions. You finish up here."

As we went downstairs we stopped on the landing and walked back to the door. I then put a finger across my lips for the vicar to listen and not say anything.

The sergeant used my phone to call the station, he said, "Sorry sir, the German student is on his way to see you and the report we're supposed to have concerning the photographs taken during professor Harris and Winters Apostle Club party. I didn't say anything about the Russian being murdered. You want me to return now? What about turning over the room? I haven't looked under the carpet yet. Yes sir."

On the way over the vicar asked, "A murder, there was nothing mentioned at the university about a murder."

"No vicar, rumor is that the two professors were involved in a drunken brawl and the university is in collusion with the police to cover the whole sordid thing up. I heard that a cleaning team from the university was used to tidy up the aftermath at the pub. One of the cleaners was supposedly telling everyone the next day about all of the blood that had to be mopped up."

"Oh dear, what is one to think?"

The chief inspector was waiting as we walked in. He escorted us to his office.

The vicar demanded, "I would like to see the report the sergeant told us about. This young man needs to get on with his studies and not be bogged down with any sordid cover up."

"I am the ranking officer here; there is no cover-up."

I wanted to drill this lying policeman, but by being humble and direct he was about to hang himself.

I said, "Thank you officer. I am happy everything is above board. We would like to see the report now so that I can have a chance to repudiate the charges that there are pornographic photographs in my possession."

The chief inspector turned beetroot red and started muttering sounds we couldn't understand.

Now the vicar was getting annoyed by the inspector's waffling.

The vicar said, "I will be informing the diocese of this crime you have instigated today."

The inspector sat down in his chair and said, "Oh what a tangled web we have woven. You have uncovered an injustice to this young man and I have been an accomplice to a dastardly deed."

"Vicar, there is more to this young man than meets the eye; he seems to have us all over a barrel with exposing a network of influential individuals. I will not be able to recover from this debacle and the mystery surrounding this student. I suppose my commission is in jeopardy."

The vicar demanded. "Someone has to clean this mess up and who better than you? We will keep this among the three of us if you promise to stop your interfering with innocent students."

"I will go back to the first day of the murder and start the investigation all over again. The co-conspirators will be summoned and be put into an official report. You are right. I must not leave this for someone else to clean up. I'll make things right. This new investigation will take months to be concluded, hopefully by the end of the school year."

The vicar wanted to know if there was a murder, then why wasn't everyone informed. The inspector was shaken with the uncovering of Volkov being killed.

The vicar and I left as the chief went back to my flat to make sure everything was put back in its place. I went to the chapel to have a cup of tea with the vicar. It was very fortunate he had time to go with me, and to witness the cover up being perpetrated by quite a number of responsible leaders in this small town.

After class the next morning Professor Winters apologized to me. I graciously accepted his apology even knowing he did not mean it, and went on my way. Professor Harris was also as meek as a lamb on one of his best days. I had a feeling my grades were going to be quite good that semester. More than one can play their game as long as it is in good taste and not blatantly criminal in nature. I wonder if blackmailing blackmailers is distasteful, or is it just playing by rules that are already set by despicable leftists?

I left classes early on Friday to meet the general at Kings Cross Station. After briefing him about the murder and the cover up afterwards, he seemed pleased that a CIA agent wasn't discovered. When I gave him the names of past and present members of the Apostle Club, he said my job was done; but going to university was a good cover. I also asked him to put Leos on the payroll as he was a help in getting the information for me.

Before leaving, he wanted to know about any ideas I may have regarding the Leipzig extraction. I did let him know that I was still working everything out in my mind first, and suggested that we get together next weekend to discuss them. He agreed and would let me know when and where. He left with the papers, and I was on my way to see Nicola.

When my fiancé noticed me waiting at the gate, she was thrilled to see me standing there. We went to a pub for a drink where she told me she got the package and that the other photographs should be ready, so we dropped by the shop to pick them up.

When we got back to her house she gave me the package with the cash in it, and the developed photographs were in my bag.

Sunday, after lunch, I traveled back to Cambridge to get ready for another interesting week. Leos was waiting at the station as I got off the train. He wanted to know what the general had said.

I said, "What a surprise, how long have you been waiting for my train to arrive, Leos?"

"I kept coming back when the London trains were due in. I have two passports for you that best describe the scientist who would like to defect. One is of Mr. Winters and one of his wife. Tell me, did the general say anything about me helping you in the future?"

"He said your first paycheck will be in your account in two weeks. Thank you for the passports, they will be helpful in getting the two scientists out from under the controls of communism and into the West. Any news from the Apostle Club?"

"Thank you for getting me on your payroll. All we do is sit around and talk about how bad America is, and how it is ruining everything from the rivers to occupied countries. They are so full of hate. I think that keeps them hanging around each other."

"Let them vent their hate. Do not become argumentative, I need you on the inside in case they plan something destructive against the American Embassy or Air Bases here in the UK."

I left to see if David was around. There should be some news from his publican. When I got home he had left a note to tell me he would be here at 6, if I wanted to go get some fish and chips. By the time he walked into my living room, I was unpacked and ready to go get something to eat. It was a cold winter's day, too cold to eat outside; so we resigned ourselves to sitting next to a hot radiator.

Since we could talk freely he started with his report. "The publican is really upset with a supposedly new investigation into the killing of Volkov. It is all over town that one of the university's cleaning crew started blabbing how horrific the scene was. Of course, you knew already since you were probably the one who started the rumor."

I told him, "Tell the publican you heard from one of the policeman and he said it was a smoke screen. No one is going to do anything with the investigation outside of drinking free beer at his pub. It was a Russian agent who was murdered; it happens to be part of the consequences of being a spy."

David continued, "There is also new information that when the two Russians were here someone turned their place over in London, and got away with 20,000 quid. The Russians were going to use that money for their operations here in Britain. When the police ripped your place apart did they find any extra money? Are you sure you are not in over your head with all of this cloak-and-dagger stuff?"

"You want out? I would understand if it is getting too scary."

"No, but you need someone besides me to watch your back now."

"There is someone besides you here in Cambridge. I have the backing of two others, with another two being recruited without them really knowing they are going to help me."

"Do you want to tell me, so I can be of help if you get in a bind?"

"No, I won't get into a bind, thank you anyway David. Take off and leave a note if anything comes up, regardless how trivial it may seem to you."

I was ready for some rest and had to study for an exam tomorrow. Hiding the money would be a waste of time. I would put it in a safety deposit box and hold out a couple of grand to use in Prague and Leipzig as a little insurance money. General Simpson called the next day to ask if Nicola and I could meet them in Edinburgh on Saturday night. A room was booked for Friday and Saturday night at the George next to Waverly Station. I confirmed we would be there late Friday evening.

Nicola was excited about the prospect of having a weekend in Scotland. I would meet her at Kings Cross where we would have first-class tickets waiting there for the 5 p.m. train.

The rest of the week was uneventful and I met Nicola as planned. When we got to the George, the general was waiting in the lounge. Nicola excused herself to go freshen up.

The general bought me a drink and said, "Anything you order in the hotel goes on your room. The embassy will take care of it. Now let's get down to business. There is a rumor that money was taken out of the Russian safe house and it could be as much as 50,000 pounds in various currencies. Were you in London that particular Saturday night?"

"Yes sir, I was, and it was 20,000."

"That's it, nothing more."

"You didn't ask for anything more."

"If the Russians ever find out who took their money, there will be no safe place to hide on this continent."

"I have two passports that need altering when you get the photographs of the assets."

"They came two days ago along with the translation of the Russian papers seized from Volkov's jacket. Do you want to know what they were all about?"

"They were about having Leos taken to Russia."

"Yes, how in the world did you know that?"

"I just wanted it confirmed, and I needed to know how they were going to get Leos onto an Aeroflot plane."

"There was another gift sent to Mrs. Thibodeau with lots of documents taken from the Russians' apartment, I believe you know about those already and they should be back and broken down in English in a week or two. We will have to schedule another weekend away."

"Was there anything else from the raid I should know about, like money and guns?"

"The guns were disposed of and you didn't ask about any alcohol that was available. I also need to tell you about me being an exchange student in Leipzig for three months, representing Cambridge."

"How did you wrangle the exchange, no on second thought, I don't need to know Wright."

"The ladies are coming sir, shall we talk later?"

"Good idea. Go to the bar and get mother a gin and tonic and whatever your girlfriend is having."

When I brought the drinks over in a tray the general said, "I will have a double Scotch and branch Wright."

"It is already on my tray, sir."

"Wright, do you pre-empt everything?

"Not everything sir, some things are best left to play out."

Nicola was blushing; we all thought it was pretty funny.

She said, "I have no idea what you mean, darling."

"I was talking about baseball, Nicola, nothing else.

The weekend went just like the cocktail hour, full of fun with a few meetings now and then between the general and me.

On Sunday morning, Nicola and I left for London just after breakfast. She needed to get back to prepare for her next day's class. I arrived back in Cambridge in the early evening. A note was under my door from David, I was to meet him at noon. He came around again to tell me that the police questioned him, and he was even less sure what had happened than when it was fresh in his mind. It was a waste of time to go over old clues no matter how honorable.

The rest of the semester was interesting watching the two professors struggle and squirm trying to deal with not really knowing where or who was in possession of the incriminating photos.

Christmas break was finally here and most of the university was in the spirit, with the smell of hot mince pies in the air around every coffee and tea shop. Nicola was waiting for me to get to Harrow as fast as I could. There was one last meeting with the general, so he could brief me on the latest news from Langley. I probably wouldn't see him again until late March if I stayed for the full three months in Leipzig as planned.

I met with Leos and David individually on my last day in Cambridge before leaving for Harrow, and eventually Leipzig by way of Prague. Leos was meeting me at the station. He would be traveling to London and back so he could brief me on the two scientists, who were waiting to defect. The instructions from me was for my two helpers in Cambridge to keep an eye on any particular odd events, and to keep a log of all left wing activities for the next three months or for the length of time I am gone.

Leos was on time and we boarded the train in first class so we could get on with business.

I asked him, "I need to know the names of the couple on the base who want to come to the West."

"They are Jifi and Iva Kroupa. Also, they are very good friends of my mother and father."

"Do they have any children living in East Germany?"

"They have one child, a daughter called Monika who is attending the University of Leipzig. We used to play together all the time when we were younger, as we were neighbors. I always wanted to see her when I went to see my mother and father."

"Could it be any advantage to have her help me with her parents or is that too risky?"

"Yes, I am sure Monika will help you, if only she could get over her fear of talking to someone about her parents. She does not like living in the communist state of East Germany, and will do anything to have the old country back."

"Can you tell me something about her that only you two could relate to, like something from when you were small kids?"

"Yes Billy, there is a funny thing that happened, but not funny back then. Monika hit my fingers with a wood mallet and they swelled up to twice the normal size."

"Please write a note introducing me to Mr. and Mrs. Kroupa; and a message from your parents saying that they love America, but they would like it better if the sun wasn't so bright every day. Do not say where they are working."

"I will do that now and we can still keep on with discussing your job of getting the Kroupa family out. I would love to see Monika over here as she is my favorite fraulein. Here is the note and another note to Monika telling her to trust you, also to keep you safe for you are my true hero Billy."

"Thank you for your kind words Leos. I am not a hero of any description. I'm just a lucky guy who has had a success or two."

"No, you are wrong, you are very brave to do what you do, and you know I could never do any of your work."

"Okay Leos, we will leave it at that, except to say I like a little excitement and having the opportunity to visit these countries after reading about them back in high school."

"We are pulling into London, Leos; thank you for the information on the people in Leipzig. This information is going to help get me through a few doors, and just maybe be the help I will need to finish my assignment. Have a merry Christmas and I will see you in about three months, if not before."

"Okay Billy, you be careful, and remember the communist authorities do not want you as a friend, only as a tool to keep the other citizens in some type of order."

Christmas in London was like no other throughout my life with seeing the Christmas lights of Piccadilly and Oxford circuses. Christmas morning we all opened out gifts. Nicola received a round-trip British Airline ticket to Garmisch from me. We would fly out the next day to Frankfurt to pick my car up from the ASA compound, and then drive to start our three-day skiing trip. She asked to see my ticket to see if it was the same.

I had to now tell her in front of her parents that I was staying on in Europe, traveling to Bad Aibling and then to Leipzig. Her mother and father were staring at me as if they wondered why I should go to a Soviet Bloc country. I would drop her off at Munich Airport to catch an afternoon flight back to Heathrow.

She asked, "How long will you be in Leipzig?"

"Up to three months. I have to do a job that requires me to go on a student exchange at the university there."

"Oh darling, what kind of job could you be doing in a country such as that?"

"I am not able to talk about my work; however, you need to know a little bit about my assignment. It is not dangerous; it involves stolen academic text books."

Her father staring at me said, "You see Flo, I told you he was a bleeding spy."

"No sir, it's not an espionage assignment, it is mainly to do with being an exchange student for a semester in East Germany."

"I know what is in front of me boy and it's not a professor."

Nicolas's mother stopped the conversation, saying, "Now stop it Jack, you do go on. Pour us all a sherry as it is Christmas morning after all."

"Well, you just be careful studying over there me old son, and come back in one piece."

After her father finished what he had to say I didn't want to take it any further, I let it go. However, the sherry was helping to avoid anymore conversation.

The next day Nicola and I flew out and picked my car up from the ASA base. The six-hour drive was fun with her in the car. At one point well into the drive she opened the glove box to see what I had in there.

She saw my pistols in their holsters; I had completely forgotten they were in there. The leather belts and holsters took up most of the compartment.

She was horrified that I needed those things. Her look was of, what else are you keeping from me?

Nicola put one pistol back in the holster and finally asked, "Why in earth would you have something like that in your car. Tell me you do not need such a thing it in your work?"

"I am so sorry you saw the weapon. Yes, sometimes I do need to have it in case I am in trouble."

"Have you ever had the need to use it?"

"Nicola, I told you there was a part of my work I couldn't explain to you. The reason I wanted to put off our wedding is that one day you would find out something about me that you couldn't handle. Then you could make the decision to marry me or get on with your life."

"Oh darling, I want to be with you forever and ever. I do not want you to be in danger that is all."

"I need to tell you something, I did not want your parents to know. My assignment in Leipzig is to bring out a couple of high-level scientists who want to defect to the West. I do work for the CIA when they need someone to do a job inside the Soviet Union"

"My father was right when he said you were a spy."

"I cannot tell you anymore about my work. One day I will. You have learned more today than you should have. You do have the right to know about the man you will marry one day, just not now; can you wait a little while longer? Once my youthful looks are gone, I will probably be let go by my country."

"Also, Nicola, as you know I may be away for up to three months. Can you go to my flat with your father to make sure everything is alright? If there are any notes shoved under the door, please store them until I return."

"My darling, I couldn't bear it if you were away from me for too long. The last time waiting for you to arrive from Germany was just so awful, with the time dragging on forever. Please be careful, I am really worried something may happen to you, knowing a little more about your work won't make the waiting any easier."

Chapter 17

The Assignment

We arrived at the Zugspitze Hotel at the foot of the big mountain, its namesake. That was where we spent our first date almost a year ago, a really special place and my favorite German town. The three days went by much too quickly, and before I knew it I was dropping Nicola off at the airport and continuing on to Bad Aibling.

I had the two passports doctored by a CIA contact in London in my suitcase. They seemed really good to me, but they still had to be inspected and approved by the ASA team. As I walked into the front door a team member came out to see who was in the office.

It was the first sergeant, "Welcome back soldier, we were expecting you. When we received the teletype Lieutenant Wright would be here this week, we all thought *who in the world is that*? The old man reminded us how you manipulate certain situations."

Captain Summerall came out to see what all the noise was about.

He said, "I should have known. My men don't get excited about anything, except you Wright. Now tell me, how did you become a lieutenant?"

"Well sir, I asked to be a captain; they compromised by granting me a first lieutenant."

"I see you are still a smart-ass, Wright. Welcome back, you haven't grown up one bit."

We all laughed with the old man slapping me on the back.

With getting back to business he asked, "We will start the briefing first thing in the morning, and then go to the woods the next day to get you across the border. I need the passports you are going to use for the assets. We also have your West German passport here under your alias of Ludwig."

"I will need $5,000 to take with me, especially if I am to be in Prague and then Leipzig for up to three months."

"That is a lot of money, Wright. We have a new general in charge and he is a stickler on paperwork, especially with money disbursements. How is our old CO General Simpson coping being cooped up in the embassy in London?

"He is enjoying the job most of the time when I don't create little problems. We meet at least every two weeks somewhere in the UK."

"I cannot fathom you being let loose in England Wright, especially in London. We are ready to close up for the day. I will go get your money and meet you and the team at the officer's club if you can get everyone in. I can't believe you are an officer. We will celebrate New Year's tonight, but still get to bed early."

We had our boy's night out, but didn't stay up late so that we would be fresh in the morning. I had to call Andrea tomorrow and set up a time for her to pick me up at our usual roadside rendezvous.

When I entered my office the next morning I found everything was still the same. *Andrea should be at home* I thought, as it was before 8 a.m.

She answered with, "Is that you Billy?"

"Yes, it is Andrea, could you pick me up at the same place in three days. It will be New Year's Day, around 10 a.m."

"It is so good to hear your voice, I have to go now; yes, yes, yes, I will be at the place. I missed you Billy."

I was leaving to get some breakfast as Captain Summerall arrived.

"Are you on your way to the mess hall? I will have to go with you as you need someone to sign you in."

"I would like the company, sir."

We were the first ones in the officer's dining room. I forgot for a moment that I was now officially an officer.

Summerall said. "I did get the orders when you got your commission, and I think you deserve your new rank. It is also appropriate that you are getting the pay that goes with the rank. You seem different. I know the jibes yesterday was to get back where we left off earlier in the year. You are always playing mind games and planning at the same time. So few people can do that, and we need those types of people in the intelligence community for deflecting any unwanted communication. How is married life treating you?"

"We didn't get married, sir; I thought it was unfair to Nicola to live another life and not confide in or trust her. I know it is supposed to be for her safety. I am torn between doing what is right and what the agency deems to be right, if you know what I mean."

"I know exactly what you are going through. That same thought process hit me before I got married. Not keeping your wife informed will in no way guarantee her safety. The bad boys want you and me, if they have to go through a wife to get their target, then they will do what is needed. I will say to you, off the record, my wife knows everything about me and my work. She knows about all of my associations."

"Thank you for telling me that sir. When I spoke to Andrea this morning she hinted that we should become more than just friends. I am going to marry Nicola one day soon, and I really didn't want to tell her about any outside peccadilloes in Europe or anywhere after we first got engaged. It is going to be tricky to pretend to like Andrea and not want to get involved at the same time. To me she is a vital tool for my survival as a spy inside of the secret police headquarters. I know you can't advise me on this as to what should be done to placate her."

"Wright, I cannot give you any advice; it is a problem only you can deal with. Remember if you forsake her and get caught, then not only does she lose, but Nicola and you will lose. The assignment would also lose with your good intentions intact. Weigh that up before you tell her no. The first priority will always be, for any covert mission to have a chance of succeeding, the fox (or agent) must get away from the hen house alive, so another attempt can be made."

"Thank you, sir. I will in the next three days play it out over and over in my mind, and will most likely act instinctively in the end."

"Back to business, why do you need $5,000? That is a lot of money in a Soviet Bloc country."

"I will tell you two parts of it. Andrea needs to be paid a little more than her monthly allowance. I am going to set up the concierge in the Jalta Hotel with stealing five $100 bills from my safety deposit box.

He has stolen from me in the past and I know now how he works. Then hopefully if all goes well, I will have him replaced with a mole of my own choosing.

"I still have almost 2,000 Czech Koruna from my last trip on me to use, until I get the dollars exchanged."

"Okay Wright, you will have the money tomorrow morning when we leave for the campsite. If there is, somehow miraculously, any money left over, you can hand it in on your return."

The briefing inside the ASA headquarters started with putting in a request for 20 rounds of ammunition for my revolver. Captain Summerall gave an order for the first sergeant to take the pistols to the armory, and have the right size cartridges and velocity appropriated for those particular weapon's use since they would be used for close-range encounters.

He went on to say, "Wright, these two passports are good, except for a few problems. Two more passports are needed with an American visa stamp if they are placed on a flight to the States. We are having copies of the photographs made for the other two passports. You will be using these to have your assets flown out of the country. They do not have an entry date and place into Leipzig. Leipzig Airport is not accessible from the West. If you could get your people to Prague for a flight to London or New York, we can have the passports ready today. The entry stamp will be dated for January 7, if there is even a little mistake on the stamps they may be excused since the New Year's festivities would have been in full swing."

"Thank you, sir, for spotting those mistakes. The assets will be in Prague towards the end of March at the latest. The two plans will work in tandem with each other, by using one flight to mask the flight that is used for the extraction, with two sets of passports to be used for different destinations. As you know some plans do not go as planned as circumstances dictate the course of change."

The captain adjourned the briefing for lunch. We were all to be back in the room no later than 1400 hours, where final orders would be cut and the schedule for the next day mapped out. Our afternoon meeting was taken over by the new general from Frankfurt. After telling us how this action behind the Iron Curtain could be more explosive than any other covert assignments outside of the Novak's defection last year, he went on to explain how there were many loose ends not taken care of.

I asked, "Please explain sir, what loose ends are you referring to?I am crawling under the wire in two days."

"Be always aware Lieutenant Wright of unforeseen roadblocks or obstacles. The wind may not be always at your back."

I was livid with his use of clichés and hyperbole for a mission that involved a truck load of danger. I had to stay focused and get to the point with very little time to go.

"General, could you elaborate on the loose ends of this mission and their consequences."

"Yes, Wright, I can to some degree. The couple in question has opposing views about coming to the West. The wife is... what is the word?"

"Hesitant."

"Precisely, thank you Wright. You will have to approach them and sell them on why they should like to go to wonderful country like America."

"General sir, how do you approach someone who is in a fortress? Most of all I have no time to indoctrinate or persuade someone to do something in the 30 seconds I have to spare to get them in a vehicle."

"Lieutenant, that particular base is even more of a fortress than it was when you successfully brought out the last two scientists. I do understand your dilemma and you have my blessing."

"Sir, the last two assets came to me by walking out and getting in my taxi, which takes away from how to get inside of the fortress. Those means of escape will be looked for by the guards in any future attempts on anyone wanting to escape."

"You excelled yourself again Wright, we are all counting on you to be successful this time. The CIA has paved the way for your success."

I couldn't believe all of that crap with the general filling my thoughts with nothing. The need to get away from his useless chatter fogging the mind was essential in getting back to the game plan.

"If there are no more questions, I will hand the meeting over to Captain Summerall as I have to leave for Frankfurt. Let's do this again after the mission is completed."

We were called to attention as the general left the room. The captain followed him out as they were seen talking beside the green army sedan. The captain was shaking his head in disbelief on what he was hearing.

With the general and old man out of the room, the first sergeant in front of the other four team members said, "Wright you have a situation, as General George Custer would have said when he was outnumbered by a force 50 times greater in his final battle."

"First sergeant, I have heard enough clichés for today."

"He was a little scary wasn't he?"

The old man walked in just in time to hear me say, "The CIA paved the way with what? It sure wasn't anything helpful to the previous or this assignment."

"Here is the bad news, Wright. The general is going to allow you $2,000 instead of the $5,000 you wanted."

"Well captain, I suggest that you give the general the $2,000 and tell him he has to do the job himself, I am out of here."

"Calm down, Wright. I already have the $5,000. The general wanted to try and get you to do the job with less money that is all. He thought if you get caught, there would be no way to retrieve the money you hadn't used."

"Is he off his rocker?"

That brought laughter from everyone. The whole team was in disbelief in the general's lack of concern for my safety. The captain had the four passports and the money, which would be given to me on the morning I left for the border fence.

The plan was as last time, for me to leave my car at the Hof Air Force Base with Summerall riding with me, and the team in the bus following. We'd camp out in the forest the night before, so that we could scout the border.

The next morning we were away by 8, and would be at Hof by 11:30. Our plan was to meet with the quartermaster over lunch and pick up box lunches for supper, and one more for my trip.

"Captain Summerall, while riding as shotgun said, "Wright, if you pull this job off, I will guarantee you will get your captain's rank from General Thibodeau in London.""

"Captain, if I am successful, I will promise to start going to church with my fiancé more often. I have a request, as soon as I get back, whenever it is, I would like two round-trip first class tickets to Tampa, Florida during spring break along with a beach house on any beach on the Gulf of Mexico for two weeks. Can you get that request for me?"

"I will say that it may be possible with the help from the CIA funding your latest assignment. General Thibodeau may balk at your request, especially the first-class tickets. One other thing is bothering me. I read a report of the agent in charge of Czechoslovakia, had an untimely death while jogging with you on the Langley farm. Can you tell me about it?"

"Sir, speak to Thibodeau about the report I handed in on that tragic episode. Back to my R and R, before putting the request in writing, have Thibodeau and his wife meet me at the beach cottage where he can debrief me on my assignment. I am quite certain he and his wife would like to join Nicola and myself in Florida."

The captain got back to the business at hand immediately as he read the quarter master's notes.

The news of the border fence was good for now, as the Czech and Russians had the 5,000 to 10,000 volt current turned off as they were extending the width of the defenses. However, when I was ready to try to cross back over in three months, the work would have been finished in the Bavarian area.

So we were on our way to set up our campsite, with everyone pitching in. We couldn't wait to get to the border, stopping to listen for workers or border guards.

That evening the captain said, "Wright, all officers have the bus to sleep in. We need to go over how you are going to communicate with us back in Bad Aibling."

"I may find it impossible to call you for fear of a tracer being put on any phone calls leaving the country. What if you were left a coded message on the office machine that the sun is going down in the West? That would mean to be at the border before nightfall the next day. If for any reason the entry point had to be changed it would be impossible to meet you that evening at a particular area. Let's think about it and discuss it in the morning.

I need to get to sleep so we can get an early start, good night sir."

Chapter 18

The Long Road to Prague

The next morning we did work out a code to use for a pick up time and date. Once again the ASA team watched me disappear into the Czech forest. This path was getting more and more familiar as I had used it several times before to sneak behind the Iron Curtain. Walking cautiously for an hour, I tried to listen for any noise above the sound of my beating heart that would alert me to danger. I was an hour early hoping to scout out the small main road leading to Prague.

In the distance Andrea was standing deep inside the woods, waiting to give me the signal to proceed. This wasn't normal as she should have waited closer to the road like she did before, so she could watch for any traffic. I had a premonition that Russian soldiers were waiting to arrest me. This was not going to be as smooth a crossing as in the past. A decision

219

to carry on or make my own way around had to be made then, not a moment later. It was beneficial she did not see me or it would have been over for both of us if she was being used as bait to trap me.

I veered off into the forest on the left, to make my way towards the area where I had left three dead soldiers and a truck in a previous encounter with a roadblock. It was going to take me the best part of a day to get there as I had to walk through the woods for cover. With lugging a small suitcase and wearing two suits to keep me warm in the freezing weather was fortuitous to say the least, but not good for running away from anyone. I ate snow to keep hydrated and munched on leftover biscuits from the boxed lunch to give me energy.

I made my way to the road as it was starting to get dark. It was safe to walk in the dark towards Cheb and then on to Prague. On the outskirts of Cheb, with daylight coming through, I found an old, abandoned barn to sleep in during the day.

The rats were pretty thick and didn't mind one more guest. They would scavenge during the day, and I would be gone when it got dark enough for them to sleep.

I started walking on the main road. I had a funny feeling that Andrea may come back to find me. Just in case, I placed a marker of crossed tree limbs by the roadside of the farm tract for her to assume I made it this far and was on my way to Prague.

The long dark winter's night gave me plenty of time to travel a good way towards the city. In basic training we marched 25 miles in 12 hours with stops in full combat gear. I figured I could walk at least 30 miles in the 16 hours of darkness. The only problem was finding an abandoned farmhouse so far from the border when the sun came up, or maybe the hotel off this road that I had booked last year for two nights. I was getting close to the little hamlet where it was located.

After a cold frosty night and with the dawn breaking, the sign pointing to the Areal Botanika Hotel by Horn I-Bezdekov was in front of me. Now if I remembered, it was down the lane towards a forest. There were no lights on or cars in the parking area, which was probably a good sign. The last time I was there an attractive young lady was taking care of the place for her parents, who were on a skiing trip to Yugoslavia.

I spotted a garden shed on the edge of the woods, and thought it would be a quiet place to sleep for a few hours. After going inside and closing the door, I peeked through a crack in the wall towards the hotel to see if anyone had noticed me or if any lights came on. Wrapping myself up in a roll of garden sheeting, I fell asleep for what seemed like a long time. Looking out again hours later, there was still no one around or any vehicles by the place.

It was time to take a chance and see if I could get a room and something to eat. I had to do something since it could be difficult to continue without any food to keep me going.

I was starting to get delusional from the freezing temperature, and not remembering what day it was or being able to work out how long I had been walking. I was still with it enough to work on a plan to help get me taken care of, if the young lady was indeed alone. The psychology of most females is that they would care for a hurt animal or person, but not trust a robust, unclean looking tramp.

After burying my suitcase under a bunch of clay potting containers, I found a broken rake handle to use as crutch for a sprained knee. A sprained ankle would have swollen up, but a knee would most likely have a small water pocket, not visible unless it was looked at by a doctor.

I walked to the back of the shed for cover and into the forest without being seen. After making my way around and out of sight of the hotel, I came out of the trees on the side where a large glass conservatory was attached to the left side of the large mansion.

I started limping towards a bench when the young lady came out with a large German Shepherd dog. It was the same young girl as before. I sat down to wait for them to come to me. The dog was growling and showed its displeasure having me on the property.

She spoke in Czechoslovakian, and not understanding I looked blank and asked her to speak in German or English please.

She smiled and answered in better English than the last time we spoke.

"You look familiar, have you stayed here before? If you don't mind me asking: Why are you here now and looking as if you are sleeping in the forest?"

"Thank you, Fraulein, for allowing me to answer you with me looking so dirty. I have been hiking and having twisted my knee, I have been looking for shelter for two days. My mother and father were booked into your hotel last year wanting to visit me at the university. I booked them in hoping they would be approved to come to Prague," I replied.

"I rode my motorcycle here and had lunch with you on that particular day. If you remember we had soup, schnitzel and pom fritz. In the end my parents could not make the trip because traveling permits were not granted to them by the Czech authorities. I went back to West Germany to see them instead while on the Christmas break."

"Yes, I remember now, you paid for rooms and never used them. Do you need a room for tonight?"

"Yes please, for two nights, I am meeting someone in Prague on Saturday afternoon at the university.

We walked into the hotel and to the reception desk. I gave her the same student ID with Herr Franz Biegler on it. I tried to pay her for two nights with meals included. She wouldn't take the money since the rooms were never used from the last time.

I asked her politely, "Could I please go get cleaned up and have another schnitzel with fries?"

"Yes," she laughed and asked, "Why do students always have pom-fritz with their food?"

"It is the most economical and fills one up at a manageable cost."

After a hot bath, she joined me for lunch and a glass of wine. Again, no one else was in the hotel.

She asked, "What are you studying at the university and how many more years do you have to go before finishing?"

"Political sciences and democracies of the world."

Jokingly I added, "I am also almost through the extended course of transcendental mind extraction from human beings."

Again she laughed with a most attractive giggle and said, "You are teasing with me."

"Let me try to extract a thought from your mind. Think of your parents for just a moment."

"Go on then."

I put my hand on her forehead while producing a low continuous hum before saying, "Your parents are on a skiing holiday."

As I took my hand away she excitedly said, "That is amazing, Franz. They are on a holiday skiing. Wait a minute, it is winter and they are not here, so you could have guessed that with some accuracy. Where have they gone?"

I put my hand on her forehead again and said, "ummmmm, they like to ski in Austria, but have gone to Yugoslavia."

As she laughed she said, "No Bulgaria, they went to Yugoslavia last year; wait I told you that last year. You are a big liar Franz."

We were both now laughing out loud.

"You told me where they went when I saw you last year. Now it is only fair you tell me your name since you have seen mine, on the registrar."

"Lenka Dagmar. Are you taking a political class for maybe the possibility of becoming a member of your government?"

The door has just been opened for me getting into her mind, on the state of Czechoslovakia being controlled by a foreign power. I had to play it out a little bit at a time.

"Lenka, my interest in politics is a psychological one on how different societies are controlled, and how some people let it happen. I believe the masses want to be able to go through life without being told what they must do or not do."

"Franz, I do wish we were free as you are in the other Germany. When our people try to protest against the Russians, they are murdered with the Czech police looking on. Do you ever protest in secret as we do?"

"Do your parents feel the same way as you do or are they willing to be controlled by the authorities?"

"You are asking questions that scare me. You may be an informer."

"No Lenka, I am for rights of the masses, not for the few. You can trust me not to be a collaborator."

"You will have to convince me Franz, I cannot take the chance with you asking questions about my parents. You have to prove to me before this conversation is started up again."

"I am taking a huge chance by what I am going to tell you. I crossed the border three days ago, and started walking when my contact agent was compromised. She was in an area where she was not supposed to be. It was a hunch or you may call it intuition that I felt there was something wrong."

"Franz, again you will have to prove you are what you say you are. Words are easy to use against someone like me who has no idea what is going on outside this area."

"Okay Lenka. I have my case in your garden shed that will prove I am not what I seem to be in your mind. Please go with me and have your dog join us for your protection."

We went to the shed to retrieve my suitcase. As we got back to the hotel, we went to my room to back up my story with a few items that could persuade her. Lenka was taken back with the $5,000 in cash and numerous passports lying beneath my clothes.

She said, "I believe now, you are different than anyone I have ever met. Last year, you were a student also and your parents were coming here to see you."

"No Lenka, I was going to use your hotel for refuge from the secret police and from the Russians."

"Franz, were you involved with the shootings last year of three soldiers at a road inspection?"

I had to think of something to say quickly before she became afraid of me as a possible killer.

"No Lenka that was the work of an American agent called Joe West; he was also killed a few months later in America. They say it was an accident while he was jogging and was possibly assassinated by a Russian Agent."

"Your way of speaking is not European. Are you an American or an Australian?"

"I am an American, Lenka. Now can we talk about something other than information I am not suppose to tell anyone. There is a need to have someone help me, as this is a good place to rest up before leaving. Will you allow me to stay for a few days?"

229

"Before answering, I want to know your real name and the reason for being in my country."

"My real name is Billy. No one knows me by that name in Prague. My contacts know me as Ludwig or Franz. I help the ones who want to go to the West and can be a benefit to the Americans. By your fear of giving out information about your parents tells me you are not happy with the Czech government and cannot trust them."

"Alright Billy, I believe you, but there are a few other questions needing answers. Where will you be next week, and then the week after that? Who are you helping now?"

"I am sorry; I have told you too much as it is. Your safety could be in jeopardy if the secret police ask you questions and you seem to them to be holding back information. They do not care about one human being even though you are attractive, to them you will be a tool to get to me and your beauty will not be of any help."

"You are right Billy. I do not like the foreign government and would like to see the last of them. You can stay for two nights as you have already paid. My parents need the money to help them pay bills in the winter or else I may be a little reticent for fear of the Stasi."

"What if I pay for a room to be mine for a year, to come and go as I please? The US government pays for a room at a hotel in Prague in advance and has been doing so for years. I have used that room in the past and would like to change hotels as soon as possible, since I would rather stay in the country but still be close to the city."

"That would be good for us; however, my parents are the ones to ask. They will be back on Sunday. Is it possible for you stay for four nights so you can speak to them?"

"Yes, thank you for letting me stay."

She happily accepted another two night's money for lodging. The rate was less than a dollar a night with breakfast. Tomorrow would be for resting, and the next day Saturday would be a good day to see Topol my Gypsy taxi driver, to exchange some dollars into Czech Koruna and East German Marks.

It was getting dark and she wanted to walk her dog before it was too late.

I asked, "Do you mind if I walk with you before we have dinner?"

"I thought your knee was hurt."

"It is feeling better after soaking it in the hot bath. As long as we don't walk too fast it will be fine. When we get back, I would like to call for a taxi to pick me up on Saturday morning to go to Prague."

"Your agent, would she not come get you?"

"She could, but someone might be watching her. She was waiting for me in a strange area and I sensed something was wrong. I have to find out first if she had the Russians with her when she was supposed to meet me, or maybe I am just paranoid at being captured."

Lenka and I went deep into the forest with her dog now wanting me to pet her. Lenka was pleased that it wasn't suspicious of me anymore.

She said, "My Sasha likes you now Billy; she is always a good judge of character."

"I am glad because she can look pretty fierce. I think we should be getting back as it is getting hard to see."

"We are heading back with doing a large circle; you will see the hotel soon. Maybe we can go for a longer walk tomorrow a little earlier. Sasha would like that."

"I would like that too; what time do you get up in the morning? If you want me to let Sasha out when I get up, if you are still sleeping I will be glad to do it."

"That would be good if you could also give her the food in her dish, which I will get ready tonight; it will be in the larder."

When we got back inside the hotel she went over to the bar and poured us each a glass of wine before going into the kitchen to fix something to eat. I followed to see if she needed any help. I was put to work peeling potatoes and washing a cabbage. After having supper we went back into the lounge and put on a rock and roll record.

She asked, "Could you teach me to jitterbug or jive?"

"Okay, that could be fun"

After 20 or 30 minutes she got the hang of jitterbugging. We laughed a few times after getting tangled up with our arms. Sasha looked at us and decided to go to her bed in the kitchen where it wouldn't be so noisy.

The song "Strangers in the Night" started playing; she put her arms around my neck as we swayed to the music. When it stopped she put it on again.

Lenka putting on the same song for the third time was more than a sign that she was becoming comfortable with my being there, and didn't mind me putting my hands on her hips. We sat down and had another drink with her wanting to hold my hand.

She asked, "How old are you Billy?"

"I will be 22 in August. How old are you Lenka?"

"I will be 20 in June. Could we have one more dance to Frank Sinatra before we go to our beds?"

As we danced, she held on to me ever so tightly and brought her lips up to meet mine. I was feeling in the mood to make love to her, but when I thought about Nicola for a moment I lost interest. I think she found me acting a little reserved rather than coming on too strong. I was actually thinking of my promise to Nicola, to marry her one day, so that was the reason to stay just friends.

After the dance I gently pressed my lips against hers and said, "Thank you Lenka for a wonderful evening. I will see you in the morning for breakfast. Do you want me to bring you a cup of coffee if I am up first?"

"Yes please, now I will show you to your room to make sure you have enough covers and towels."

In the bedroom she looked to make sure everything I needed was out in the appropriate place. As she was about to go to her room, Lenka stopped and kissed me again, this time with a lot of passion. It felt good to be in her arms and having her fingers caressing my hair. Our bodies pressing against each other, we slowly fell onto the bed, where we continued to hug and kiss as if we both could not stop the passion. After a long steamy session of embracing, Lenka fell asleep in my arms. I took her shoes off and covered her up with the heavy quilt. Thankfully she went to sleep, no telling what the morning after would have been like if we had made love.

After waking up first, I quietly crept downstairs to let the dog out and make us a cup of coffee. On my return she was still asleep, so I left the coffee on a bedside table and went back downstairs to feed Sasha. The dog was eating as I looked around for eggs, bread and bacon. I almost forgot. Europeans like to have a boiled egg, cold cuts and cheese to go with their thick, grainy toast. Soon I had put it all together. Finding a tray to put her breakfast on, I took it back up to wake her and give her the breakfast.

Her first words out of her mouth were, "What happened last night Billy, were we naughty?"

"No Lenka, we were close but not dangerously so. Here is your breakfast and Sasha has had hers."

"I should have brought you breakfast, you are the guest. Do you have a girlfriend in Germany, or is that a silly question?"

"I had a German girlfriend and now have an English girlfriend who I met in Mannheim. Do you have a serious boyfriend?"

"My parents would never let me go out with a boy until my 20ᵗʰ birthday. Thank you for being a gentleman last night. My father would thank you for not taking advantage of me."

"I would never take liberties in the heat of the moment. Now saying that I did enjoy being close to you Lenka, you made me feel a little nervous when we were caressing each other. I will go and get you another coffee, and then let you eat your breakfast."

"Bring your coffee back and join me, we can talk some more. I want to know all about you and where you grew up."

As I was making more coffee a car drove into the front of the hotel. With the way Sasha was wagging her tail, the noise of the car's engine had to be one she recognized.

The couple let themselves in and saw me starting up the stairs. They were startled to see me in the house as the lady ran up the stairs. She called back down in Czech to say something; the man wanted me to stay where I was. Lenka came out of my room to tell her mother she was glad to see her.

This did not look good in front of her parents. The mother came downstairs with her husband to confront me for being alone with their daughter in the house. I waited to let the three of them work out the awkward situation.

Lenka was giggling and persuaded them to go into the dining room for coffee and to hear her side of the story. Again, I kept quiet and out of the way. After a half hour the father came out to the kitchen to have a word with me. His English was good along with his German; he asked which language was my choice.

I told him "English please."

He stridently replied, "English is good. I want you out of here today and to never come back."

"I am sorry sir. I have paid for four nights in advance. However, I will be ready to leave tomorrow morning."

He left the room, and I went outside to walk around the gardens to gather my thoughts. I had to make sure he didn't call the police and put me into a position of doing something regrettable. Lenka came outside to explain her parents' attitude.

I asked her, "Please do not tell them what I am doing here for now. If they get to know me better then we can tell them more."

"Billy, we will all have dinner tonight and then you can win them over. That will be your only chance. My father used to be a soldier in the Czech Army and will not be easily swayed. I told them you acted like a gentleman last night and could have taken advantage of me. I told them I wanted you to, but you were not going to. Papa was impressed by me telling him the truth.

Billy, my father will not let you stay because he knows how close we were last night; he thinks it would happen again if you stay."

"Your father is very wise and it may be better if I go tomorrow. I would assume he would not like me to book a room for a year in case I come back for a visit."

"We will ask him and ma tonight. Who knows, he may get to like you. You two have so much in common, wanting to help free our people. He doesn't like the Russians or their helpers. Let's go walk Sasha in the forest and be alone."

It was nice being away from the hotel and her parents where the atmosphere was strained to say the least. I don't think Mr. Dagmar would be happy having me too close to his daughter. I really couldn't blame him.

That evening we all pitched in to get the dinner ready. I was in charge of preparing the vegetables while the ladies cooked, and her dad laid the table and opened a couple bottles of wine.

I was glad to be in the kitchen away from her father. Her mother kept staring at me and managed a smile a time or two. This was a fairly good sign that she was warming up to me being in the hotel, I hoped.

Chapter 19

Foreign Exchange

As we sat down for dinner I waited to help with Lenka's chair and likewise her dad got his wife's.

Mrs. Dagmar said something in Czech and the father replied, "Tonight, my darling, we will speak English for Billy's sake or Franz or whatever his name is. Why do you sign in as Franz and my daughter calls you an American name like Billy?"

"Mr. Dagmar, I have several aliases in my line of work. I am an agent with the American intelligentsia out of Frankfurt and Washington."

"You are putting us all in danger Billy with your being here. If the authorities find out we have knowingly harbored an American agent we could all be shot."

"Mr. Dagmar, I have you and your family's interest in mind. I will leave tomorrow, and will not put this house in jeopardy again. I am sorry for the inconvenience I have caused all of you."

Lenka spoke up, "Papa, what about Billy's safety? He is willing to help some of our people out of the country without thinking of the danger he is in. No wonder the Czech's have been a slave to two different totalitarian governments for the last past quarter of a century without ever firing a shot in defending themselves."

Her father looked like he had just been caught with his pants down. He knew she was right; it is safer to turn the other cheek no matter how hard your assailant strikes you.

I quickly answered Lenka by saying, "It is different for your parents; they have roots here, and could lose everything including their daughter. Whereas I do not have these restrictions and I can flee or use force if I have to without retribution. There are different and smarter ways to fight an enemy, such as giving refuge to an anti-establishment provocateur, which does carry some danger."

Lenka's father still looked sheepishly as he showed his true colors in front of his only child.

He did reverse his indifference on my being in his hotel as a guest, but definitely not as a suitor for his daughter.

I had a feeling he didn't mean it and that could be a dangerous situation when he wanted me out of the way. On the other hand, paying for a room by the year in advance may be too good of an opportunity to pass up. There is an old cowboy saying "money talks and bull excrement walks" or something like that!

I went back to a being more subservient by saying to him, "Thank you, sir, for your invitation. However, I must be off tomorrow to get on with what has to be done. I would love to stay to spend time with your lovely daughter, which would only delay the inevitable chore I was sent here to do."

His solemn expression had turned into one of relief by my not wanting to stay past tomorrow. He offered to give me a lift to wherever I wanted to go. Of course I accepted, as I needed to be dropped off at the garage where my motorbike was.

We all cleaned up after supper and then withdrew to the lounge for a nightcap. I excused myself to get ready for bed. Lenka came up to say goodnight.

She followed me upstairs to tell me, "Billy, I will see you later on tonight."

"No, Lenka, we must not see each other in our rooms as my work depends on me staying alive."

Lenka giggled as she left to go back down to spend time with her parents. I went to sleep pretty quickly and after an hour Lenka crawled beside me and wanted to start where we left off the night before.

I told her, "If your father catches us he will kick me out of the hotel or even worse he could call the police."

"Oh Billy just kiss me, papa is asleep. Please take me tonight as I am yours to do with as you want."

"I am engaged to another, with hopes of marrying her in the near future."

Nothing seemed to matter with Lenka. I was on a mission and whatever it took to complete the assignment I would have to do. I had liked her from the beginning; but still it was wrong of me to not consider Nicola, even though the assignment had to come first.

The next morning, when I woke up, Lenka was gone. Her mother brought me in a cup of coffee and asked if I wanted to stay a few days longer. Of course I declined her invitation, saying again the reason was the same as last night.

It was hard saying goodbye to Lenka after what had happened. The drive with Mr. Dagmar was quiet as he obviously did not want to talk to me, but he got me to the garage along with my suitcase in one piece.

While getting out of his car he asked, "When will you be back Billy, I was wrong with not welcoming you into our home. You still have two nights paid for on your return."

"I would love to go back to your hotel, maybe in the middle of March. Tell your lovely wife that I think she is a good person as is your beautiful daughter."

The garage mechanic remembered me and went to get my motorcycle.

I asked the garage attendant, "Have you seen Andrea lately?"

It was hard to understand him in his German and Czech translation. He still thought I was German.

He managed to say as he smiled, "She will be happy you are back in Praha, Deutschlander."

The bike looked like it was polished down to the spokes. We tried to have a conversation, but with the interpretations of three different languages it was hard to keep a dialogue going; so I paid him 100 Koruna for looking after the bike. He motioned it was full of fuel and ready to go.

As I was driving out from the forecourt a policeman drove in staring at me. He came after me squealing the tires of the small funny-looking Lada or Skoda. I turned bike around to leave the town through a back cobblestone street. It was icy and hard to keep the bike upright. The cop car was having just as hard a time and then he sideswiped a building and ran head on into another building. Looking back, I saw there was smoke or steam coming from his car, and he was in the middle of the road shooting at me.

I turned down a pedestrian pathway and headed for the Gypsy market to hide the bike and myself. When I got to the gates of the market I jumped off and walked it to Topol's tent. He was so glad to see me as he gave me a big bear hug. I motioned for him to hide the bike and told him the police were looking for me and must not see it.

The big Gypsy asked, "You will be staying with the Gypsies tonight here at the market, no?"

"Yes, thank you. Could you get me to Leipzig tomorrow or Monday? I will need to have the Leipzig clan help me in February or March. Will you be able to exchange $3,000 into East German Marks here today?"

"Tomorrow you will exchange dollars with Leipzig Gypsies. It is better we go tomorrow with so many drunk Russians and police still celebrating. Next day they may wake up. Is good, no?"

"Yes, that is very good. I would like to have you take my motorbike also, maybe in a trailer. Later on after we get to the Gypsy village and change the money, I will need to have you wait outside the base where we waited last year. Before we start the mission I have to go to the university halls to check in. The time frame for all of this could be within a couple of weeks or several months."

"Yes, good, I understand all of this. I don't think it will be possible to enter that fort. They will shoot you on sight, English. Waiting on the street is good, no?"

"Yes, that is good. If it difficult for a stranger to get in, what about an ambulance getting in late one night or early in the morning, would that work? Perhaps we can pay money to one of the guards or drop off a bottle or two of vodka and come back maybe in an hour to see if they are willing to help us, or even more desirable, are passed out."

"Yes English, the vodka is best. They would share with all of their comrades and maybe the officer in charge. Yes, ambulance can go anywhere."

After sleeping under the Gypsy cart all night, we were off at dawn. Topol's daughter was home getting ready to go back to college. She was the only one who interpreted my conversations last year as she was fluent in English. She had taught her father a lot since then.

Topol wrapped my bike in several horse blankets and tied it on his roof. He first drained the petrol tank and wrapped the engine with an old, dirty blanket. Now we were off to Leipzig traveling on back rural roads so to evade any suspicious policemen.

Five hours later we pulled into the village just before noon. After getting the bike right side up and exchanging the dollars, I gave Topol a good day's wage. He was happy and asked for me to make sure to plan to stay with him and his family in March for a few days.

I set up a plan with the Gypsies on how we would get into the secure base where my assets were living. This was going to happen in about two months time if everything worked out. We hoped to get an emergency vehicle inside and with the help of the two scientists' only daughter, we should be good to go.

I left for the university with a bunch of bulky black market East German Marks stuffed inside my pockets and sweatshirt. Finding the school was easy with having directions from the Gypsies where it was safe to drive the motor- bike far from the police station.

When I finally got to my hall of residence, a porter was waiting to take my German passport. After he got me to sign for bedding and two towels with his higher than me attitude, he handed me a number that had to be pinned to my washing bag every Monday.

He looked like a man who couldn't be trusted with his scowl and prying eyes. I handed him a 10 mark bill for a tip. That turned his scowl into a big, toothless grin. I would call him smiley from then on; he had earned that coveted title.

In my room on the second floor, and with the door closed, I wedged a chair under the handle for security reasons. I had to see if a camera and a listening device was in-bedded somewhere.

The room with its sparse furniture made it easy to locate one camera. It was in the corner of the high ceiling where the chest had to be moved to reach the offending mechanism. One of the wires had to be put out of commission. The listening device I left alone so maybe the camera would not be fixed with having at least one eavesdropping device still working. After my alterations the chest was replaced in the same spot, and now it was time to look for a hole or loose floorboard to hide my money.

A bundle of banknotes and passports had to be hidden in at least two different places, along with a good stash under clothes that could be found easily by the secret police or the porter, which should satisfy their curiosity.

The passports for the two scientists had to be as secure as the money because that was their safest way out of the country. It was also important to study their names, so I could locate their daughter here at the university. The last name "Kroupa" was an easy name to remember; however, the parents had to use aliases to leave the country.

I was about to hide the passports in the bathroom when I spotted a small camera alongside the ceiling light. Good thing the light wasn't working or the brightness would have blinded me. I would not have noticed an extra bit of metal on the side of the round ceiling holder, which was white.

I decided to leave it there and went back to the bedroom to hide most of the money in the tubular bedstead on the bottom by taking off a hard rubber pad and replacing it in a way it could not be easily removed again. More money was put in my chest of drawers, and another lot to be kept on me at all times.

With nowhere to hide a pistol and holster, they had to be part of my dress. I went downstairs to tell the porter my bathroom light wasn't working. He followed me back upstairs with a bulb in hand, and asked me to carry the heavy wooden ladder. When he finished I pulled out two vodka bottles out of my top chest drawer and gave him one, and put the other one on the top of the chest to signify that it was mine; and to keep everyone out of my room.

I was about to say something when he stopped me and pointed to his ears with pinching his lips to say someone is listening and pointing around the room. I shook his hand in a way to tell him *thank you*.

Smiley left with the ladder and had a much larger grin this time with his cheap hooch. I am sure he thought this poor lost soul could be eavesdropped on so easily.

With paranoia sinking deeper into my mindset, I moistened a strand of hair onto the outside of the door when leaving to see if anyone went into my room. I wanted to make sure the porter knew about my motorbike. He went outside with me so I could show him the bike in the coal shed. Now he was taking care of me as planned.

With my bike safe, I started walking around the area to get familiar with the new surroundings. Finding a cafe where students hung out was the highest priority before looking for Monika Kroupa. The closest place to the university was a few hundred feet away. After going in the cafe I asked two young female students if I could join them at their table; they obliged and seeing they had very little coffee left I bought them another when I went up to get mine. They were overly pleased by my generosity and scooted closer to me.

We were getting acquainted with introductions when Professor Winters walked in with his wife. I muttered a typical American colloquialism. The two girls looked at me and asked if I was from America. By their reaction, one could tell that they were hoping I was. When my answer was yes they enthusiastically welcomed me to Leipzig. As one could tell from my reaction to Winters coming in, I was not happy to see him. With him and his wife joining us, I couldn't ask these two girls any questions about a student called Monika.

The professor's wife asked sarcastically, "So you are the infamous Ludwig Von Wilhelm I have heard so much about."

With that the two girls got up to leave, they had a look which said: *You liar, you are German, not an American.* At least they took their coffees with them to another table and didn't throw it on me.

Mrs. Winters asked again, "Oh dear, I am sorry, did we break up your little group? You waste no time in finding women, do you Ludwig?"

With my displeasure of having them join us, I replied in a deep Southern accent, "Yessum, I told them two pretty girls I was a first cousin to Elvis Presley."

"Ludwig, you do a fantastic impression of a Southern American. I am impressed."

"Mrs. Winters, I likewise am impressed by your quick wit to go along with your stunning beauty."

Professor Winters was not amused by his wife enjoying our banter. He interrupted us by getting up to leave.

She said to her husband, "Not yet darling, I'm starting to enjoy Ludwig's humor and his looks are likewise appealing. Now, go ahead darling, you wanted to ask Ludwig some questions."

"Not now please, there will be plenty of time to take on this impertinent individual, who or whatever ever he is. Wait, yes there is something bothering me. How did you get to Leipzig, did you crawl under some wire and sneak in, I am sure they would have refused you after I..."

He stopped himself before divulging that he tried to have me denied access to East Germany, and left quickly with his wife sitting at the table looking bemused.

I asked her as I pulled her chair back so she could leave, "Will I see you later ma'am?"

"You are quite the confident boy, aren't you Ludwig," she said as she gave me a gentle slap.

If looks could kill, the professor would have finished me off as he stared at me through the plate glass window. He was seen telling off his wife quite harshly for a supposedly gentle left wing appeaser who is supposed to be for equal rights and all of that stuff. It was funny to see him so upset over me getting the best of him. Now to track down Monika to see where she lived and the classes she had signed up for.

I went to the admission office to see who my lecturers were, and to try to talk my way into seeing Monika's schedule. There were several young female volunteers that seemed to know what they were doing as they were busy shuffling papers and talking to new students. After studying them I asked the shyest girl to see what my schedule was and that of my friend Monika Kroupa.

A nice-looking girl standing next in line, made me look like a complete fool when she said, "Vas ist los?"

I answered in English, "You are not called Monique Grouper as well as my friend, are you?"

It was lucky she was quick enough to know I was a foreigner and answered in English, "You called my name, no?"

"Yes, I may have as I believe we have a class together with a British lecturer."

"Herr Winters is your professor also?"

"Yes, he is from Cambridge, I believe?"

"That is correct."

"Is it possible to take you out for a drink?"

"Yes, it is possible when we are finished. You English are much faster than our local boys getting to know the Frauleins."

"Monika, do you believe in luck in meeting new people? I do believe that luck has a lot to do with one's future. Since I am an exchange student and do not know my way around, can you take me to a good place to have a quiet drink?"

We will go to a student hang-out and see if any of my friends are here today, if that is good."

She took me to a cafe that served meals, and was a favorite gathering place for university students. Monika took me over to a corner where she could see who was outside on the sidewalk. The cafe was quiet so far, but filling up fast.

I had to confide in her before I lost her in the group, or if someone called me out on not being a German.

I said, "Monika, I had to approach you; it was an accident we met at the registering in counter. I would have found you sooner or later."

She had a petrified look as she got up to leave.

"Wait Monika, please let me explain. I have a note from Leos for you to read while I am in your company, and a note for your parents."

"Leos who?"

"Novak"

The other customers were starting to stare at us as she grabbed my hand to leave without finishing our drinks. We hurried down the sidewalk away from the university. Coming to a small park she sat me down on a bench.

She asked, "Who are you and what do you want of me? I have nothing to say to you."

"Monika just listen to me and I will explain what I am doing here. One of my assignments was to follow professors Winters and Harris to Prague University. They are Russian agents and are here to gain you and your friends trust in them.

"Monika, you must not be taken in by them, and please tell your friends not to be fooled by them either. We know all about your parents and that they are needed here in Leipzig for their work on rocket and space propulsion. The Russians want to guarantee that your parents stay put and do not defect as the Novak's did. Please Monika, ask me anything before dismissing me altogether."

"Please show me the notes now or I will have to walk away."

After handing her the notes, she started reading them, laughing and crying at the same time, as she asked for a handkerchief as she studied her prized correspondence.

She read the notes over and over again for quite awhile. Waiting was making me nervous as the police or some collaborator could walk by and find this situation strange with her crying and me looking worried.

Chapter 20

The Leipzig Connection

Finally Monika said, "Welcome to Leipzig Ludwig, whoever you are. Leos loves you, he says you are his hero."

"Monika, Leos as you probably know, has been in love with you ever since you were children, and after his hand became normal again after you hit it with a wooden mallet, he soon forgave you."

She was crying tears of joy now knowing that Leos was alright. She was starting to regain her composure as she said, "Poor Leos, is he in America with his mother and father?"

"No Monika, he is at Cambridge in England; we are both attending the university there."

"Thank you Ludwig, for telling me these things, are you here also for another purpose?"

"I was told your parents want to go over to the West, but that your mother may have to be persuaded to leave."

"Mama does not like to talk of such things because she is afraid of the secret police. Mama will be hard to convince."

"Like Leos you are vulnerable not only for your opposing views about the establishment, but you are also needed here to make sure your parents stay. Harsh as this may sound Monika, the Russians may want to relocate you to a university far away to ensure your parents are going to stay put. But you could join Leos in Cambridge, and go to the same university with help from the American government."

"How can you prove all of what you say is happening or going to happen? I have thought many times of escaping and would come to realize my mother and father are more important than my own selfish freedom."

"Call Leos today if you can keep the answers short as your parents will tell you everything. Go talk to them as soon as you can, and they will tell you that they also think like you do. The Novaks and your parents used to talk in private of their plans to leave the country as soon as they could."

I then told her, "One very important thing that is happening now is that one of your group is actually a spy for the secret police. Think, over the next few days, who you would suspect to be the one."

"One of my friends working for the Stasi, it is not possible. I have been through all the schools with them."

"Monika, I can only go by what has been told to me. You may be right, but if you are not, one of them will follow you to the base where your parents work. Let your friends know when you are going to visit your parents; and then let me know so I can see if anyone follows you. Do not let on if you are followed, let me deal with the problem."

"What can you do Ludwig? You are so young and less inexperienced I am sure than the Stasi."

"I will take a photograph of the one following you. That is all I would be able to do."

"Alright Ludwig, I was planning to see mama at the market on Saturday morning, and the go back with her to see papa and have lunch with them. I am sure no one will be following me."

"Okay Monika, could you meet me back here in the bar Saturday evening or Sunday morning at the other cafe?"

"Yes, I will see you here around 7 p.m. Until then Ludwig, thank you again."

After leaving Monika I went back to my residence to see the porter and make sure he was being good. The porter, seeing me come through the door, came out from behind his counter and handed me a note. I smelled the pink envelope it was in, as he signaled to me it was from an attractive older lady.

I stopped just in time to inspect the door to see if anyone had intruded into my space. It appeared no one had, unless the camera in the hall picked up my actions and replaced the hair. Next time there would have to be another way of finding out if my privacy had been violated.

The note was from Mrs. Winters. *"Dearest Ludwig, it was an intriguing encounter we had in the cafe when my husband and I walked in to join you and your two girl friends. Meet me at the same cafe this Wednesday for lunch, about noon. I'm looking forward to our next meeting, yours, Steph."*

What a stroke of luck meeting up with the professor's wife and I hoped to be able to get inside her home and have a look around after a few more meetings. The next morning after the first class, I went to a perfume shop with Mrs. Winters note to have her scent analyzed, or a sniff test applied by the perfumer.

A shop specializing in upscale lady's apparel and perfumes was on the High Street. The young lady, after smelling the envelope, said in German that it was an expensive product called L'Air Du Temps; and that they did sell it. I bought it in an atomizer that had an art nouveau design.

The translation was fittingly "something is in the air" and no matter the cost I thought it would pay off. I hoped Mrs. Winters could give me an approximate date they were hoping to go back to England. Then I could get the Kroupa's on a flight a day or two before the Winters left, by going through Prague.

On Wednesday morning I took my motorbike out of the coal shed to go by the base where the assets were living. Stopping a block from the area, I let a little air out of my front tire then I continued on and stopped at the front gate to check out the bike's tires while seeing if the guards were aggressive or armed. This was essential in planning the extraction. The two guards approached me and asked what I was doing there. I pointed to the front tire and told them it feels like it needs some air. They looked and agreed it should be seen to.

The guards were very young as this was probably a boring job, which needed soldiers who were not as athletic or particularly astute in being a soldier. At least that was my impression based on past experiences from being in the US Army for three plus years. Their rifles were World War 11 vintage and were most likely bullet free since there was no magazine or ammo pouch on their belts. The important observation was that they were fresh looking and did not seem tired, indicating the changeover was within the past hour.

Across the main thoroughfare and next to a slip road, a sign with an apartment for rent was inside a second floor window. After pushing the motorbike across the empty street I knocked on the door, and after awhile a sleepy old gentleman came to the door. I wanted to inspect the place he was renting. He asked me to come back later as his wife was the one to see. After telling him I just wanted to inspect the place, and then if it was what I wanted I would come back to put some money down. My German must have been getting better as there were no reason to repeat myself.

I couldn't believe my luck, it was ideal with a full view of the front gate. I asked him if there was a place to park my bike or could it be kept in the room. He shook his head no; it would be good in the work shed out back. He mentioned his wife would be home soon, as she worked the night shift as a cleaner on the army base. She slept all day and worked all night.

His wife came in as we were about to go out to look in the shed. I told her I would like to rent the flat for a year as I was going to the university, and the rent seems cheaper away from the town. She then gave me the price, which was way too much. I started the negotiations with a price of half what she was asking. After she said no, I started to walk out the door. She stopped me and came down to almost half. We finally agreed on a price, and she had a smile on her face that told me it was still too much.

I shook my finger at her and said "you are too smart for me."

The three of us laughed as she pulled me into the kitchen to have a shot of snaps to seal the deal.

After paying for a month's rent in advance, I left and said I would move in on Friday afternoon. With the black market money exchange, the rent worked out to be about $5 a month. The real exchange rate would have made it three times that amount. Next, I needed to get some old used German Army clothes and boots to make it easier to blend in; it would help in deflecting anyone becoming suspicious of a stranger moving into the neighborhood.

It was time to head back for my first class. Harris and Winters morning classes were typically boring with both of them routinely flirting with the German Frauleins. Occasionally they would glare at me as they did not want a witness to their dalliance with much younger girls in case something was said back in Cambridge.

I was in the cafe 30 minutes early so I could eat enough to fill me up, and then order something light to eat in front of Mrs. Winters. The waitress had the table cleaned up as she walked in.

I said, "Mrs. Winters you do look lovely, and I have been nervously waiting to see if you remembered our lunch date."

"Ludwig, please call me Steph or Stephanie. Nervously waiting doesn't fit your demeanor, Ludwig."

"Stephanie is such an attractive name. That will suit me very much if you don't mind. I brought you a little gift for our first date."

"Ludwig, you shouldn't have. How did you know this was my brand? You are a clever young man."

"How long are you in Leipzig for Stephanie?"

"We are here for three bloody months in this bombed out dump. I may leave before our time is up, and let him stay behind to flirt with the young girls or boys or whoever his interest is on a particular day. He is going to take a few students on a field trip to Moscow in two weeks, to the Karl Marx Museum."

"Why would the professor want to go to Moscow in the middle of the winter, and how in the world is he getting there?"

"He's a bleeding communist and the Russians are arranging transportation for him and three students, probably all young and pretty little girls."

"Why don't you go Stephanie and help him in his work? He may need someone to keep him on a schedule."

"He doesn't love me or want me around anymore, and I don't care much for him. If it wasn't for his good wages I would have been long gone. Besides, he is going to meet up with his new contact from the Russian Embassy in London. I really get up his nose when he is called a bloody commie by me. He told me the trip was going to take two weeks and possibly three. What do I do for two or three weeks?"

"Stephanie, I have to get back to class; can we see each other again later this week?"

"Yes, Ludwig, I would like that very much. Come over to my place for lunch on Friday. Thanks again for my perfume, don't bring me anything when you come over."

I now had the professor's address and his schedule for the next four to five weeks. His real purpose for this exchange trip was highly suspicious, maybe a clandestine planning session. My next meeting with his wife was going to be interesting to say the least.

Back in Winters' class on Thursday, he asked for three volunteers to go on the field trip. I held up my hand as he started picking only young women. He stared at me as to say *"sorry old boy you are out of luck again."* He picked the three most attractive girls and the fourth prettiest as an alternate. The professor apologized for not taking everyone who wanted to go, and said there may be another trip planned during the Easter break. Of course, he was due to leave before Easter to go back to England, the fibbing toad.

I met Stephanie at her flat for the Friday lunch date. We started with a glass of wine before the meal. I asked if it was possible to be given a tour around the flat and, of course, she was glad to do it. When we got to the spare bedroom, which was made into an office for her husband, I finished my wine quickly so she would get me another one. While she was gone I gazed at the papers on his desk and saw a large brown envelope addressed to the Kremlin with the name Vicktor R.

Mrs. Winters called me to come down to the dining room for lunch. I read the Kremlin correspondence as it was in a rough form of English, and it was about the new KGB agent assigned to London and a replacement for him. I had to copy it, so I called back down to say I was going to the bathroom to get washed up. In there I copied down the name of the replacement KGB agent. It was Vladimir Phouten, who was to travel on March 28 and meet the Winters at Heathrow Airport in the afternoon.

As I was coming down the stairs she was starting up to see what I was doing. She heard the front door open as we were about to sit down.

Stephanie said, "Bloody hell, what is he doing home? Quick Ludwig, hide in the kitchen!"

I whispered, "Calm down and pretend you had lunch ready hoping he would come home for a change. Put your apron on and go give him a kiss so it will distract him; otherwise, he may know something is up."

I could hear him say something and he went upstairs to his office. She came to the kitchen to get me to leave. Outside, I was relieved and thought it was quite funny that we were almost caught by the teacher.

Everything was working out as I moved into my eavesdropping operation center, the apartment across from the base. Now with my suitcase and old German Army clothes I could walk around the area and not feel out of place, especially with the Russian fur hat with large ear flaps to keep me warm.

That afternoon after moving in, I started cleaning the motorbike. The old man came out and saw I had a bottle of vodka to keep me warm. He grabbed a cloth and started wiping down the back spokes. As soon as I handed him the bottle to have a drink, his wife came out and laughed at us saying our dinner was on the table; she was going to work.

We both went inside to wash up. He poured us both a glass of wine to wash down the stew and a lump of hard bread. After supper we both went out to put the bike away. He asked if I wanted to go to a guesthouse for a beer. I declined and said something like "another time since I have to take a bath and get some rest."

Three hours later I pretended to be tipsy and wobbled across the street to where the guard shack was at the front gate. One guard came out to see what was going on. I gave him the bottle to have a drink as the other guard came out. They left their rifles inside the gatehouse.

They both helped me finish the bottle as I fell into the guard and took keys from one of the guard's belt loops as we went tumbling to the ground. After taking his keys, I stumbled down the road and doubled back to my apartment to make notes and watch the two guards. They acted quite drunk. Although they were different guards from the other day, they were also young and looked like new recruits. At midnight an army vehicle pulled up from inside the compound to change the guards. An officer got out of the small vehicle to inspect the gate, probably to see if it was still locked.

After going through the keys, I took the one that seemed the most likely to be the gate key. I stumbled back across the street at about 2 a.m. to place the unwanted keys next to the curb by the gatehouse.

As I pretended to fall down and leave the keys, a guard came out to shoo me away. I offered him a drink, before taking it he looked around to see if anyone was watching. I started to stumble away when he took the bottle from me and told me to get going as he put his right boot against my back side to push me onward.

Again, I stumbled down the same road and as I did before to get back to my flat without letting them know where I lived. Back inside the bedroom, I watched as the two guards finished the bottle. Then it became quiet over there without anyone coming out of the guard shack to check if anyone was trying to break in or out.

I finally went to sleep only to wake up as the landlord was knocking at my door. I opened it to see what was happening; he asked if I wanted breakfast and seeing how rough I looked he laughed and left me alone. I started watching for Monika to show up to meet with her mother.

After awhile she came up to the gate for the guards to let her in. A young- looking man walked up a few minutes later to talk to the guards. They seemed to know each other. I took plenty of photographs and even one with him hiding on the other side of the gatehouse when Monika and her mother walked out of the gate. The two guards' photo was taken with the stalker laughing as he almost was seen by Monika.

I went back to sleep and woke up a few hours later, around noon, in time to see Monika walk into the base with her mother. The same young man that I had snapped several pictures of earlier was also let inside the compound. That was an interesting situation depicting he must be either military or KGB. It conjured up several problems on the chances of getting the scientists out of the base.

Monika finally left to head back towards the university. A different man was now on her tail. I took several snapshots, hoping one would be clear enough for Monika to see if she knew who he was. Since he came out of the secured base it was the same scenario as the younger stalker. Now we had two agents to be on the lookout for.

At least it was known now that the bus stop was being used for getting to and from this area.

I went downstairs to make an appearance for the landlord's sake, so they wouldn't think they had a recluse in their apartment. The back garden needed some attention with broken bricks and broken roof pan tiles scattered all over the place. It may behoove me to get on the wife's good side by clearing up the mess.

After working for an hour the lady came out to give me a cup of coffee, and she asked if I had a headache. I laughed and told her I was good, just in need of some fresh air. She appreciated me cleaning up the garden as her husband was unfit to do such work.

It was imperative to be looked on as a good young man by helping around the place. Maybe they would let me eat with them when I was there; she was a good cook going by the stew she made yesterday. After another hour the place was looking better, and it was then too dark to work any longer. I went back to my flat to go over the notes and arrange them in an order of the events as they had happened over the last five days.

This flat would be a much better place to hide the money and passports, especially if I replaced the lock on my main door with a tamper proof one. That would probably mean keeping the place in the hands of the CIA for a few years.

I went back to my dorm to get out of these old clothes and meet Monika. The porter asked why I was dressed like that. I told him about helping some old people to clean up their garden. When I entered the room a note was on the floor, but there was no sign of anyone opening the door. Mrs. Winters note read, *"Dear Ludwig, I did enjoy our quick liaison the other day. Please meet me here again on Monday for lunch. P.S. The perfume is such a lovely gift. Stephanie."*

The scent was overpowering, which should mean something is in the air. I left the room and arrived early to meet Monika and have her wine ready before we got something to eat. She was on time and looked pleased to see me as her smile indicated.

She greeted me with a kiss on both cheeks and said, "Hello Ludwig or should I call you Billy?"

I could feel the heat rise to my face from the panic I must have showed. There may be a need for me to leave town. I was speechless, at a loss for words for the first time in months.

"Don't worry. I shouldn't have been so blunt Ludwig. I am so very happy for no real reason."

"Monika, I see the cat is out of the bag. Please call me Ludwig from now on. How did you come by the name of Billy?"

"My mother and father, of course, were told everything by their friends who you had helped escape from the horrible base. I thought of what you said about one of the group who could be a Stasi officer. There is one who seems to never have a class with any of the other members. No one followed me as far as I could see when I went to take ma to the market."

"There was a man that followed you to the base and inside of the complex. When you left to go home, another man came out of the base about 30 seconds later and waited until you boarded the bus, and he then ran to catch the same bus."

"How would you know all of this. I didn't see you following me or anyone else. You are starting to scare me Billy with not knowing anything about you or who you associate with. You could have been told all of this by a Stasi or making up the whole story to get me to trust you."

"I took some photographs of the two men and I will have them developed on Monday or whenever I can get them done. You then will be able to tell me who they are. The secret policeman who is part of your group must stay in place. The devil you know is better than the devil you don't, or the one he is replaced with."

"Ludwig, give me the film to have developed by a friend in the university as I need to know if you are telling the truth."

Chapter 21

Undercover With Monika

Monika was still a little nervous with letting Billy Wright into her life, not really knowing anything about him. That was about to change, and at the same time, so was her life forever.

"Billy, where do we go from here? My parents are convinced you are the one to trust to help them defect. I would have to leave for the West as well, or the Stasi would hold me for ransom to get them back into their laboratory. Some of my friends are coming into the bar, you will have to go. Let's meet tomorrow morning for coffee at the other café, and I will show you around Leipzig. You will tell me everything tomorrow about you, and how you knew I was being followed."

"Yes, I will tell you everything, goodbye until tomorrow."

I stopped at a store to buy a few bottles of vodka, two on the cheap side and one good bottle for my room. The porter was just coming downstairs when he stopped me to say something about Mrs. Winters. We were rudely interrupted by a policeman in uniform asking for Ludwig Von Wilhelm's room. The porter lied and told him he was moved to another building by the university office.

Smiley said, "He will be back, you better leave now. I know this man and he is evil, maybe the older woman's husband turned you in or told them a lie to get you taken away for a few weeks. It doesn't matter who they take, no one ever returns."

I thanked him and gave the good bottle of vodka to him, and then left after I collected my money and clothes.

It was dark and getting to my new digs was going to be tricky, but at the same time it was fortunate no police could see I was moving house. The porter said he would keep any correspondence for me in his office. Before my next meeting with Stephanie, I hoped to have gone over everything in professor's office.

Both of my landlords were home and curious why I was still moving stuff in. I explained that my girlfriend has kicked me out of her apartment for good. As they invited me in for a drink, I gave them a bottle of the cheap hooch. I don't think they were impressed with their present; they sort of turned their noses up when they saw the label.

After a sleepless night I met up with Monika for coffee.

She said, "You look like you have been drinking all night and are in need of some sleep."

"I do need some rest after moving my stuff to another location last night. A policeman stopped by the dorm to make inquiries about me; it was lucky I was downstairs and was a witness to how mean he looked. The porter lied and said that Ludwig Von Wilhelm had moved to another residential hall.

"How much notice do your parents need to leave? They can only take one piece of luggage each. Go see them this afternoon and have them leave all of their personal effects, including photographs in their apartment for a friend to pick up later.

"They are not to tell a friend or anyone about picking up any boxes until they are on the way out and only then they can pass a note under the friend's door, which would be better. I will make reservations for them to go to England on Wednesday morning on a British Airway's flight."

"Billy, I am sure that is too soon and more upheaval than they can stand in such short notice, but I will try to convince them."

"Good. You and I will leave the same day for West Germany, Monika. The plan is to have an emergency vehicle go to your parents flat at 5 a.m. You will be inside the ambulance as a nurse."

"Have your mother call the front gate for an ambulance as your father will be having a heart attack and his doctor is meeting them at the hospital. I will meet you at the airport with the tickets, and the papers needed to get them out of the country.

"Go tell the man you suspect was the one following you and another friend at the same time, that your father did not seem well yesterday, and you are going back to see them now. Say you will see them at school tomorrow."

"This is all so sudden Billy. I am trusting you with my life and my mama and papa's life also."

"It is better to have this happen quickly so no one will have a chance to jeopardize the mission. Meet me tonight at our usual place at 8."

I now had to wait until that night to see if Monika could talk her parents into leaving in three days. That would give me time to go to the Gypsy camp to see about implementing our pre-arranged plan. The first stop had to be my dorm to catch up on any news from the German authorities. I asked around for the porter, and was told he was taken away for questioning by the secret police; the consensus was he would never been seen again.

The Gypsies were expecting me as one of their clan had heard an American CIA agent was loose in the university somewhere. They insisted I stay with them until I had to leave. I agreed to stay for three nights, and they would have Topol there tomorrow morning. They had located an ambulance that a clan member drove, and it would be ready for service any night after midnight. That was perfect as they told me they would discuss the price with my taxi driver from Prague.

I left to clear out my apartment and return with all of my money and documents after seeing Monika. Back at the flat the old man was glad to see me again. I gave him money for my rent for the next 11 months, as I would be using the place off and on for that period of time. He seemed to understand my aloofness, which was comforting.

Back at the Gypsy village I was given a bedroom in a house at the back of the camp, in case they were raided by the Stasi. It was getting late and I had to meet up again with Monika at the cafe bar. When I got there she was sitting in our corner. She had a glass of wine on the table for me.

I was itching to get to her answer about her parents.

She said with a lot of excitement, "They will be ready, and your plan is so brilliant they know it will work. I will also be ready with my case packed and ready for a new adventure Billy."

"Monika, you are not to have any luggage in case there is chance you are being watched. Go stay with your parents Tuesday night, and have them ready to go no later than 5 a.m. Wednesday morning. I will be at the airport by the time you get there. After your parents have left, we will then start our trip to cross over to the West or do what needs to be done to help in our escape. There will be a nurse's uniform in the ambulance for you to put on. It will be tight and revealing if you need to distract the guards; however, the guards should be well into a couple bottles of vodka by then."

Monika was finding it hard to say good night, knowing everything hinged on the ambulance getting into the base and out again without being stopped. I had to get back to the Gypsy village to get some much-needed sleep. She also knew there would be no sleep on Wednesday morning, and we both had to keep going until we reached West Germany, hopefully before dark that same evening.

After a good nine hours sleep, I went to the airport to buy two round-trip tickets to London under the names of Winters. There was too much going on to waste time having lunch with Stephanie. I knocked on her apartment door, and she appeared in a gown with flowing sheer wings. She had had a few nips as she smelled of Scotch and wanted to have a cuddle. I broke the news that her husband had turned me in to the police and I had to flee the dormitory.

She went off on a tangent saying, "I will get my own back with that bleeding scoundrel."

I had to play her for information as she was ready to hand over the crown jewels, so to speak.

"Stephanie, did you in any way mention to your husband I was here the other day?"

"Yes, he asked me if anyone had fumbled with the papers on his desk, as they were out of place. In a fit of jealous rage I said that one person fancied me and it was young Ludwig. He said he thought you were not what you seemed to be. The no good two timer said you may be an American agent. Is that true, are you a bleeding spy?"

She downed another glass of Scotch and fixed herself another without asking if I wanted one.

I had to ask her again, "Are you going to stay here with Professor Winters or are you going back to England early?"

"No, the bugger is so into himself he wants me here to answer his letters and keep his appointments. Do you want to see where he hides his dirty little secrets?"

She took me by the hand to his office and pulled out a secret drawer on the front of the desk that looked like heavy carved paneling. She knelt down to pull the papers out and gave them to me as she closed the drawer, so her husband would not know they were missing anytime soon.

She asked me to leave as she knew I had what I really wanted and it wasn't her that I fancied. I was glad to leave as Topol would now be at the camp waiting for me to show up.

With all of the professor's incriminating papers on his relationship with the Russians and the home office, in the CIA's hands soon, no excuse could be made by Whitehall for having the **Cambridge Papers** in Washington.

Then I was on my way back to the Gypsy village with the important papers.

The big Gypsy was glad to see that I was still in this world, and he gave me one of his bear hugs. We all sat down at the dining table and started talking business and eating at the same time. There was no etiquette as to what implement should be used correctly in which hand, as we only had forks and steak knives to carve up the poached venison.

It wasn't long before money was leaving my pocket securing the emergency vehicle and the taxi. I mapped out the plan again with a different twist. The ambulance would bring the Kroupas back to the village to have the taxi take them to Prague Airport. The pickup inside the base was to be done by 5 a.m., sooner, if possible.

I asked the taxi driver, "Is it possible to be at Prague Airport by 9 a.m. if you got away by 6?"

"If we took the quickest route it would be plenty of time. We should really be traveling while it is dark so the police would not see us. Maybe leaving by 5 a.m. from here would be better."

"What if the ambulance met us at the border? Would the guards let an emergency vehicle through? Perhaps with a bribe?"

"No Billy, they would suspect something for sure. We can go part of the way and get off the main road and cross into Czechoslovakia on a small country road. That would add an hour to the trip, but it is safe. The airport is this side of Prague by 20 kilometers, so maybe we could be there by 10 a.m."

"Okay, we will do it your way, which is probably safer. I will follow on my motorcycle far enough in back of you to be an escort if some type of diversion is needed. Do you have a way of buying a nurse's uniform for the daughter. Tomorrow, have the price I need to pay for everything, including for the added help. One more thought before I go to town… would it be possible for someone to drive to the cutoff point on the main road to make sure there are no police waiting in any lay by, or to see if there is a road block is set up?"

I went back to my apartment to speak to the landlord while his wife was at work. He was glad to see me, especially after I put a full vodka bottle on the table. The information I needed was good, no one had suspected me or the drunk handing out vodka to the guards as something out of the ordinary. He mentioned that his wife thought I was a little strange, but basically a good boy with wealthy parents. Who else could dress so bad and get away with it or really not care about his appearance, except a rich man?

I had to use my apartment again to observe the changeover of the guards and to ply them with vodka. Watching and waiting was certainly boring, but it was essential to the plan. Nothing new happened as the changeover was done and I ventured out at 2 a.m. to act the drunk. After stumbling over to the guard shack and knocking on the door to wake them up, the reaction was what I suspected. They were really annoyed and pushed me away as I tried to hug one of them. He took the half empty bottle and told me to get on my way.

By the time I got back in my room they were seen finishing the bottle and tipping it up to get the last drop. Another hour went by before I went over to see if they were asleep. I peered into the window and saw they were both fast off. I tried the large key that I had stolen the other night on the gate lock. It worked on both gates: the one going in and the other one going out.

I went back to my room to get ready to go to the Gypsy village so that I could sleep all day. Topol was waiting for me with a cup of strong coffee. He gave me the total I needed to pay, which was really fair. I went to the house where my bedroom was and returned with the money. He understood that sleep was needed and he wouldn't see me again until the evening.

Topol said, "English, you work in a strange way, please never be my enemy, I don't think I would live to see my grandchildren."

"My big Gypsy friend you need not worry. I like good people who do good things for others. You are one of the best. Now have a good day, I will see you in eight or nine hours."

When I woke it was dark outside, which gave me a fright for a second as I was groggy and did not know the time. I hurried to the house where Topol was to see my newly formed crew. The ambulance vehicle was there along with the nurse's uniform, and my motorcycle was washed, fueled and ready to go.

After going over our strategy again with everyone involved, I decided to go to the apartment to start putting my plan into motion. The first things needed were three bottles of cheap low grade vodka, one for the landlord and two for the guards on the gate. Sounded like the start of a nursery rhyme, that thought did sound amusing.

The old man heard my motorcycle pull up and came out to see me. He probably suspected there was a bottle of vodka for him.

I asked him, "What does your Frau like to drink? I would like to go get her something. You and I are always having something, now she should have her favorite tipple."

He thought long and hard, after what seemed a lot of minutes, he had a big smile and said, "Yes, yes, she likes French champagne, we never buy it, too many marks."

I walked to the closest wine shop, which was block away. They had what I thought was a good selection; however, they were all covered with a layer of dust. The shopkeeper gave me a deal since no one spent over one mark on a bottle of wine, two bottles for the price of one. Now the landlady can drink one tonight and save the other for a special occasion. I needed both of them to be asleep or out of it before 4 a.m. That was for the aftermath of the extraction, when hopefully no one could give a description of the vehicles involved.

The old man was over the moon by my generosity and invited me in to share his rabbit stew. That was a welcoming invite since I hadn't eaten a thing all afternoon. The more he drank, the more he cursed the Russians and local authorities for giving in to

L. A. Wiggins

the communist regime. He wished now he and his wife had gone to the other Germany.

I left the old man on his own to go up to my flat and get ready. I dare not risk going to sleep, even for a few hours. After awhile the landlady came home earlier than normal, as I watched the front gates for the guards to be changed over.

They all looked so young as did the officer of the guard, which coming from me was sort of funny. It was after midnight with the time to act drawing nearer and my stomach started nervously churning as if the rabbit had come back to life and was trying to get out. One thing was for certain, I wasn't going to need a toilet later on that day. It may be to my benefit, smelling like a dirty drunk.

Chapter 22

The Extraction

In my old smelly German Army clothes, I stumbled down the road and back on the side where the guards at the gate could hear and see me. After pretending to fall over the curb and landing against the guard shack, the two soldiers came out to see me off. They confiscated my two bottles of vodka, which I had in both hands with no caps on them. I was told to get away as they held their noses and laughed as I fell backwards and wobbled back from where I came.

Back in the apartment and in the dark room, I watched as the guards were drinking out of each bottle. With very little left to drink they retreated back inside the hut. It was less than two hours to go to before the ambulance showed up. I strapped the gun holster around my chest and checked to make sure the bullets were still in the chamber, with another 15 spare cartridges on the belt.

A nervous tummy was now causing me all kinds of bother, especially with the minutes flying by and it was soon to be game time. That was a similar feeling one got before the first snap in their first high school football game. I had to be not only alert, but to let the adrenaline help keep me focused.

By the time the ambulance showed up I had the gate opened with the guards passed out. I quietly closed the gate as the ambulance with its lights drove off into the compound. After quietly closing the gate, I unlocked the other one and left it slightly open. As I waited, the time was now going very slowly by.

Finally, the ambulance came out and went through the gate with Monika looking out the back window. After again quietly closing it, I ran across the street and walked my bike down the road about 50 yards before starting it.

With catching up to the ambulance I followed about a quarter of a mile behind, until we ended up inside the Gypsy village. The three passengers got out to get into Topol's taxi with Monika coming over to me on the bike to give me a hug. I think the smell of the uniform was too much for her.

Monika said, "This is so exciting, even mama and papa seem to be energetic for the first time in years. Why do you smell so terrible Billy?"

"The smell is on purpose; now please keep your parents calm, especially if you are stopped by the police. Now we must go, tell your parents when we are on our way, in about an hour that we are going to Prague and not to worry."

"Why Prague, Billy?"

"I will tell you later, now you must get into the taxi."

The taxi pulled out as I was thanking the ambulance driver. After hugs from my new friends, I jumped onto the bike to catch up with the assets. We were almost an hour ahead of schedule. It was still dark with no one else on the main road to the border.

The taxi pulled into a lay by where a car was parked. I stopped at the entrance as our driver got out and walked to talk with the occupants. He got back into his taxi and started off again. It must have been the Gypsy scouting out the road ahead. Instead of going into the layby, I got back on the main road so I could keep up with them, trailing about a half mile behind.

At the next exit the taxi turned off and headed down a very small rural road in the direction of Czechoslovakia. We traveled another hour before crossing the border on what looked like a farm track. We were halfway to our destination as we eventually got back on a main road. It was now getting light and the taxi was gathering a little more speed.

Finally, at the airport, the three passengers got out of the taxi. The taxi driver told me to follow him and to park my bike in the parking lot. After that there was no time to spare, I ran back to the terminal with the two passports and up to the Pan American ticket counter.

After purchasing the tickets Monika and I walked her parents to the gate lounge. We rehearsed their new name, Mr. and Mrs. Winters; they were going to America on a holiday. Her parents were so excited to be going to New York.

At the gate I asked if the two could be pre-boarded as they had been traveling for many hours, and if they sat down they would find it hard to get back up. Reluctantly they let Monika and I walk them into the plane.

When we sat them down I stopped at the cockpit on the way off the plane, to tell the pilot, "Do not for any reason come back to the airport if you were radioed to come back. Go to Frankfurt if you are worried."

By the way I looked and smelled the Pan American pilot probably thought I'd lost my mind. My hair was dirty from riding in a dust cloud for 100 kilometers and with my face was probably as dirty.

I took out my red diplomatic passport and whispered, "I am a CIA agent and you have two high value assets that are needed in Washington tonight. When you are airborne contact your own flight control in New York and have them talk to a General Thibodeau in Washington or to the Vice President. I repeat, do not come back here."

Now to set up the rest of the plan in case we were found out. After going up to the Lufthansa ticket counter, I paid for two one-way tickets to

Frankfurt, with cash. I was now suspected of flying someone out of the country illegally. There were two red flags: one was paying in cash and another not purchasing a round-trip ticket. They asked for my parents' passports, which the ones without visas were handed to them. The flight was leaving in two hours, and the ticket agent was told my sister was bringing our parents to the airport. They seemed to be satisfied as they kept the passports until the passengers arrived for their flight.

Monika had to wait another 30 excruciating minutes. She waited in the gate lounge as I headed for the bathroom to take off a set of clothes and wash up.

When I got back she asked, "Where did you get a change of clothes, you look completely different?"

"I was wearing two sets of clothes; this suit looks more like I should be looking in an airport."

"Billy, I could never do what you do. I am so nervous. I have to go to the ladies room now."

When she left, I walked back towards the main terminal to see if anything was happening. It was quiet and got back just as Monika was walking to the gate, as the plane was being pushed back away from the ramp. We went outside to the observation deck with no one else out there because of the cold. We could see the taxi driver talking to someone.

Monika put her arms around me and asked if I would keep her warm. She then kissed me and pressed her lips against mine for a long time. I thought this is the girlfriend of Leos and I cannot afford to upset him; he knows too much about me.

I hugged Monika as the plane took off and we headed towards Topol. The guy he was talking to was a Gypsy from his village a few miles away. There was a spot of bother back at his house, with the secret police asking questions.

Topol said, "It is best you go and I will see you again soon I hope. You are a good and brave friend. Take good care of your girlfriend. I can see she likes you. My daughter thinks you are nice also if you ever want to join our clan, you are welcomed."

"Thank you my friend, tell your daughter I think she is nice, too."

"Monika and I will wait for a few more minutes before we go to make sure the plane doesn't come back. I will not be back for some time, maybe next New Year's. Here is 500 Koruna for my next trip."

"That is good English, until then, do not take any prisoners. I know you won't."

Monika and I left for the border; we should be there just after noon if I stepped on it. We were past Cheb, approaching the area the three soldiers were shot exactly a year ago. There was another roadblock on the long stretch of road I could see about a mile away. It was pure luck the sun reflected off the windshield and caught my attention. I turned down a farm track to the right and headed into the forest, into the thick woods by a kilometer or two. We got off the motorbike and started pushing it.

Monika asked, "Why do you look worried Billy."

"There is a roadblock; we have to walk around it. I think it may take us at least an hour to get past them, then if we are lucky we will be able to get back on the road. We will still be on schedule to meet up with our transport back into West Germany."

Monika asked, "How does anyone know where we will be, Billy."

"I hope my boss in America will call the boss in Germany to let him know I am coming in."

I didn't want to alarm her by telling her we were walking parallel to the East German border, and had to be careful not to venture anymore to the right.

After an hour we started gradually slanting back left on our walk towards the main road. It was difficult with pushing the bike around trees and fallen limbs. The time was going by too fast as we had to get under the border fence before dark. We were finally at the road, and I went to see if the roadblock was behind us. Thankfully, it was and could be seen way off into the distance.

We were only 30 minutes from the path to our new crossing, the one between the two abandoned farmhouses and where Andrea had been waiting when I crossed into the Czech Republic. We started pushing the bike through the forest again; but as we were almost at the border, I smelled cigarette smoke. I stopped and whispered to Monika to not say anything or make any noise.

We pushed the bike off the path and into a thicket, and covered it with pine needles. She crouched down behind the debris and was told not to make a sound until she saw me again. I went back to the path and laid a limb on it to mark the area, and then stopped to see which direction the breeze was coming from.

Someone was at the border. I gingerly made my way close to the fence where I watched until another cigarette was lit. After crawling under the fence, I could see the first sergeant talking to the captain. I bust into them with my gun in my hand, but with the safety on.

The two team members didn't know what to do - run or be killed.

The first sergeant said, "Christ Almighty Wright you scared the excrement out of me, you crazy SOB."

The captain joined in with, "I am going to kick your ass when I can catch my breath and quit shaking, you insolent so and so. You are now back to being a private.

I had to kneel down on the ground as I was laughing so hard with tears coming out of my eyes.

"Look, sorry about that, but now I have to go back and pick up someone special. By the way, I smelled your smoke a half mile away, and knew it was American cigarettes being smoked."

Chapter 23

Saving Monika

I hurried back to the border fence to get Monika and bring her finally into the West. While crawling under the barbed wire, I heard Monika crying out for someone to stop doing whatever they were doing. My heart was beating as loud as it had ever beaten before. I knew my greatest fear was happening that she had been discovered by Russian or Czech soldiers, and that probably a guard dog had found where she was hiding.

With no safe options available, it was time to hurry to see what was needed of me, before she was injured or killed. Two soldiers were too busy trying to get her clothes off to notice me surveying the situation from the far side of the path. I had to think fast, where was their truck and the German Shepherd that always accompanied the border guards? Even though it was very hard to wait and analyze the situation, it was imperative to have the edge as I had to take them by surprise.

It was extremely difficult watching her fight them off and screaming while I waited behind a tree; however, it had to be done. A frigging Russian officer ran up to see what was going on and quickly joined in with grabbing her feet to pull her onto the ground.

A bigger problem was a dog being controlled in the distance as a soldier was walking it back towards the main road. The dog was looking back wanting to help out his master. During this time I pulled the pistol with a silencer out, and took the safety off while taking my boots off. Then I started sneaking quietly towards the three men in my thick wool socks.

Monika noticed me as I was on them about two feet away as she started to lash out and scream to keep the soldiers distracted. Two rifles were laying on the ground next to the right side of the three soldiers. One soldier had his trousers dropped to his ankles and was only interested in Monika as the other two were excitedly watching. With three quick shots to the back of their heads from two feet away, the three soldiers were dead by the time they hit the ground.

When I went to gently pulled Monika up, she had her eyes tightly closed and was in shock as she had a dead soldier half on top of her. She started lashing out whereever she could find a place to sink her nails into. After striking her with an open hand, which was necessary to bring her out of a state of shock, she finally sank into my arms with tears running down her face.

At that moment I heard someone running towards us. While propping her up against the motorcycle, I asked her to stay put and not make a sound and assured her that she would be protected. I pulled the officer's pistol from his holster, for backup.

After leaving her to make my way back to the path, two men were running up from the border direction. The two pistols were quickly cocked and ready to fire on the unknown intruders as I hid behind a tree a few feet from the path.

What a wonderful sight, it was the captain and the first sergeant. How glad I was to see them and not more Czech or Russians soldiers, which would have been big trouble.

The captain whispered after surveying the carnage, "Wright, do you not ever take prisoners?"

I ignored him and asked if he would take care of Monika while I got ready to get out of there; but she wanted no part of anymore men in uniform, and only wanted me to help her. The first sergeant grabbed the motorbike as the captain led the way back towards the border.

They helped me get Monika under the wire and on the way to the bus where the other team members were waiting.

At the border, the captain noticed I wasn't wearing any boots and asked "Where are your boots soldier?"

"I didn't notice they were not on my feet sir, with all of the goings on. Please take Monika to the bus with you and I will go back to get them."

When I got back to the side of the path and sat on the ground to put my boots on, another two soldiers came up from the other way to discover their dead comrades.

One of them was wearing a Russian uniform with more decorations than I had seen before. They were frantically looking all around and through the forest to see if anyone who did this was still in the area.

Now hearing a vehicle slowing down about a mile away on the main road, I knew I couldn't stay hidden forever, especially with the dog somewhere. I stepped out from the two trees hiding me to ask if they were looking for me. This startled them to say the least hearing someone speaking English.

As I put my left arm in the air with the pistol barrel pointing towards the sky and my right hand holding the other weapon behind my back to hide the other lethal gun didn't seem to matter. The Russian officer had a look of panic and was contemplating something other than having me surrender.

I said softly in Czech to keep anyone else from hearing me, *"Vzdat se. (I surrender)."*

He was thinking on what to do a second too long; and by the time the Russian reached inside his jacket to pull his pistol, my bullet found its target in the middle of his forehead with the gun in my right hand. The other soldier was fumbling with his weapon and as he was panicking, he dropped it. I was only now a few feet away from him, and I motioned for him to turn around. He hesitated and seemed to want to try and grab his rifle again, which was a huge mistake as I put two rounds into his chest from the other Russian's gun in my left hand. He was going to be able to live before he made that fatal mistake.

My one last job was to strip the officer of his entire uniform and his weapon before hurrying back across the border. With having three pistols, I had to wrap them up in the officer's jacket to hold them while running back to the border. I could hear a vehicle coming closer from somewhere and a dog barking over the noise of its motor. When I got on the bus breathless, I ordered the first sergeant to get out of the area as fast as the bus would go because a squad of soldiers was closing in on us fast.

The old man asked, "We heard several shots back there, what was that all about?"

"I will tell you later sir, if you don't mind."

"We were thinking about coming back, but with no weapons we would have been in the way."

"Good thing you stayed put as it turned out. All I can say is it was a nasty situation."

The captain let it go at that as we were hastily retreating from the area.

When Monika saw how happy everyone was to see me she started to smile, especially when they all commented how brave she was.

With the loaded bus and the bike, Captain Summerall ordered the buck sergeant to drive us to the base quickly to get to my car.

He said, "Drive Private Wright's car back to Bad Aibling while the first sergeant takes over driving the bus."

Monika was holding on to me very tightly and asked if I was only a private.

"No Monika, I am almost a captain and my captain up in the front of the bus is my boss and doesn't know when to stop teasing me."

With that we were all now laughing as the first sergeant stopped inside the Hof Air Force Base to come back and give me a hug.

He said, "On your next mission you must be more careful, you are thought of a lot, by all of us. It took awhile Wright, but you are definitely family."

"What next mission first sergeant?"

The first sergeant was now getting a little humorous, which would be the first time he had strayed off his narrow little path. Monika was now fast asleep.

The first sergeant whispered, "Don't you wake up that pretty little girl, if you do you will have hell to pay, even if you become uncomfortable, you let her sleep."

When we got to Bad Aibling ASA Headquarters, the captain was tapping me on the shoulder to wake me up. I forgot Monika was still wearing her nurse's uniform. No wonder the Czech and Russian soldiers couldn't get her clothes off easily with the uniform made of thick denim. Someone had put a green Army wool blanket over us while we were sleeping.

Monika was taken over to the first sergeant's quarters for his wife to look after her with providing clean clothes and a bath. They were to meet us over at the mess hall for supper as soon as possible.

I had some questions before the ladies joined us; and they had, I am sure, some for me.

With me talking first I asked the captain, "How in blazes did you know I was crossing back over today?"

"General Thibodeau received a phone call through Pan Am Flight Control that a CIA agent in Prague ordered an airline captain to deliver two high priority packages to New York International. These orders were from the Vice President of the United States. You do have some gall Wright, by invoking false instructions from the White House. Now tell us what happened to have you come back early again from your mission."

"The ladies are walking in, can we discuss it at tomorrow's briefing."

"They were almost at the table when Summerall said, "Almost a captain... that will be the day Wright."

We were all laughing when the ladies chairs were held for them by way too many soldiers getting in the way of each other.

The first sergeant's wife said, "Agent Wright must be here, everyone is happy again."

The food wasn't all that great but the company was, with old stories of the boy agent who wasn't afraid of officers or the communist soldiers. Monika stayed at the sergeant's house while I slept the rest of the evening and the night away.

I was awakened the next morning by the captain. It was the first time I wasn't at the mess hall for breakfast before anyone else.

He asked me, "When was the last time you had any sleep? You and the girl, I heard, were out for the count."

"I know sir, we have had a rough two days and having to shoot those three soldiers put us both over the edge."

"Tell me Wright, why did you have to shoot them?"

"Well sir, two men were trying to hold her down with the other man had his trousers on the ground looking to get some nookie. I don't think they would have appreciated me telling them that they shouldn't be doing what they were thinking of doing."

"I see Wright, you may have a point. What were the other shots we heard when you went to get your boots?"

"Sir, two soldiers discovered their three dead comrades lying next to each other and after a few seconds they saw me after I put my boots back on and stood up. I had to kill them or they would have killed me."

"Why would you take one of the soldier's uniform Wright?"

"The officer's uniform had the look of something different from the other ones in my locker. I would like to know what rank the Russian was in case I may have the need to impersonate another Russian officer one day."

"I can tell you Wright, your hunch was a good one. He was a full bird colonel, one rank from being a general; however, you may need to gain some weight to fit into his trousers."

"Enough of this for right now, Wright, since we have to debrief the young lady this morning, and have her call her parents to tell them that she is safe and doing well. She may feel you need to be in the room; however, as you know, it isn't exactly the procedure.

You will have to tell that pretty young girl you will be close-by or in your office where you will be making your phone calls to the generals. Now let's go and get some breakfast before they close down the chow line."

The captain was enjoying eating in the noncommissioned officers' dining room. Everyone was joking and pretty loose before we had to get down to the tedious job of being debriefed.

The captain said, "Everyone, it is time to go back to work. The bad news is the new ASA general in Frankfurt will be here momentarily to witness these proceedings. Now I know you all have different views on him and are judging the new general by comparing his ways to General Thibodeau. You must not telegraph your feelings when he asks dumb questions. Let's be tolerant of General Winston Warren Woodcock, and please no funny remarks like did you hear any woodcocks while you were in the forest?"

Back at the ASA headquarters Monika walked into my office as I got up to greet her. She was extremely glad to see me and gave me a kiss on both cheeks. I wanted to sit her down and make sure she was going to be relaxed, and have her feel at ease before going into the debriefing.

I said, "Monika, what I have to tell you is what I told Leos and his parents when I brought them here for the first time. Tell them everything that has happened to you since you first met me. Good and bad it does not matter, they still want to know. Tell them how awful it was when you saw me shoot those three soldiers. They are not interested in how much you appreciated me getting you and your parents out from behind the Iron Curtain. I will be in my office if you need me; however, I have a lot of phone calls to make. Can you do this by yourself?"

"Yes Billy, I think so. You will come if I call, won't you?"

"I will be there before your last word is uttered."

At that moment the first sergeant came to get Monika and she reluctantly left with him.

After two long hours she came into my office and said, "They were all so nice Billy, they made me call mama and papa, we all cried together on the phone.

Papa said they were very tired, but having a good time with your friends Mr. and Mrs. Thibodeau. I was told this afternoon I will be going shopping for new clothes, but I have no money."

"Everyone thinks you are so brave to have done what you did. I was listening for you to call out to me if you had to. You will not need any money Monika, the ASA will pay for everything. Here, take these marks for your walking around money and when you buy a purse you will have something to put into it."

"Two hundred marks is more money than I have ever seen at one time. I cannot take your money."

"Monika, it is not my money, if you don't take it I will have to hand it in and spend time filling out a report."

The old man and the general met the team briefly in the conference room, after Monika had left the building to replace some of her personal effects she had had to leave behind. We were told to get some lunch and be back in the room at 1300 hours for my debriefing. We were not to discuss any part of the assignment outside of that room, no matter how trivial a topic may seem.

After lunch, I was back at my desk calling Nicola to tell her that I was going to be back in England very soon. Her mother took the call and told me that Jack would pick me up.

She said, "I will tell Nicola your good news, where are you at the moment?"

"I am in West Germany; I hope to see you all in a few days, goodbye ma'am." I couldn't afford to give out any more information.

It was time to call Andrea and ask her what went on at the border and if she had been alone. Her phone rang several times before she finally answered it. She sounded like she was half asleep. It was in the early afternoon, and that seemed strange since she was always on the go by 9 a.m.

She weakly said something in her Czech language.

"Andrea, you sound a little tired, are you okay?"

"Billy, it is nice you call. I thought you may want to forget me. Please forgive me for the soldiers at the border waiting to catch you."

"How many soldiers were with you? How did they know I was coming over that day? Can I call you at another phone where it will be safe to talk? I heard a click after you picked up the phone."

"Give me your number Billy; I will call back you in a very short time where the phone conversation won't be listened to."

The phone rang within three minutes. "Hello, Lieutenant Wright speaking."

"Billy, it is so good to hear your voice. You answered the phone as an officer, I had no idea you were a soldier. We must hurry because this is the neighbor's phone; you know the one I look after. There were maybe a dozen armed soldiers and a high-ranking Russian office hiding in the trees to capture you. They suspected that you were the one who killed the soldiers last year at a roadblock.

"Billy, Mr. West called the concierge at Hotel Jalta to tell him you were coming over as you did last New Year's Day. My friend, the concierge, asked me if I was going to meet you, when I said yes he turned me over to the secret police. There was nothing I could do after that, I was held for over a week and had to get back to take care of my mother and father. I had to tell them everything. Never come back on that day again. Billy, are you coming back again to Prague, I want to see you again desperately."

"You are right Andrea, that day does make it seem like a pattern. I will make sure the next time we will meet at another place and at another time.I really can't say when because keeping you safe Andrea is my first concern. Mr. West will not be telling anyone anymore of my movements as he is gone for good. If there is a need for me to go to Prague, I will make sure we get together. Washington has allowed me to set up an operations center somewhere behind the Iron Curtain. I want you to be part of the future plans, but I cannot tell you too much at the moment."

"Billy, is it possible to call you at this number?"

"No Andrea, I will try to call you at least once a month from now on wherever I am, which will not be here for a long time. Please stay safe and keep your job with the secret police, so we can possibly use their services to gather secret information on a person called Markus Wolf. Also, any information on Leipzig and Prague operations the Russians deem to be top secret. Pick up and save any micro film or hard notes that are discarded."

"Billy, the concierge is now gone because you did not show up. He hasn't been seen since the first week of the New Year. I felt you were close Billy in my heart, were you?"

"Yes Andrea, I was close, I saw you were in a different place in the forest than before and instinctively knew something was not right. Remember Joe West is no longer alive, I am now in charge of our ops in Prague."

"Before I go Billy, I do hope you will you come back soon. Also, the man at the garage said you had picked up your motorbike. I was so happy at the news I kissed him, which made him jump."

Andrea was laughing as I told her goodbye, with the image of the garage mechanic getting a kiss.

Chapter 24

Another General Sent Packing

The first shirt shouted down the hall, "I want everyone to be in the main room before the general arrives with the captain."

We all dutifully obliged, even though officially I was an officer, the team still saw me as one of them, which was how it should be. We were given instructions by the first sergeant on how the general was going to conduct this debriefing by the book, with no hyperbole or humorous jibes. I gave the first sergeant an envelope with $10 it for him to give it to the captain.

It was a good thing he was lost for words because the general walked in and the first sergeant had to order us all to snap to attention.

The general insisted on being in charge of the briefing as he said, "Well men, you all have

323

accomplished a difficult assignment. There will be a letter of gratitude placed in all of your files and another streamer added to your colors. Thank you, from all of us in Frankfurt."

"Lieutenant Wright as for you soldier, I have read your commanding officer's report and the five shootings of those unarmed men was a senseless act of violence. There will be a letter of dissatisfaction and a recommendation for you to be busted down in rank. I want to know what were you thinking as you gunned down those men. It seems that people die when you are involved in an assignment in Eastern Europe or stateside. We have to nip this in the bud, now. Our country cannot afford to upset the Russians with your foolish actions; this type of behavior has to stop today and I promise you it will if I have anything to do with it."

His statement was unnerving to say the least. I had to stand up slowly in order to gather my thoughts for preparation to defend myself after having been caught completely off guard. My waiting was bordering on insubordination. This deliberate delay had to be seen by the general as a little more than rude. It really didn't matter to me at this time as I needed to think about what had just been uttered by this cliché espousing buffoon. I was still stunned by his scathing remarks.

As the general had read from prepared notes, it was clear to me his thoughts were premeditated and he couldn't care less what today's briefings showed. I still had to quickly think on how to handle his accusatory summations of my assignment.

I was still in shock and abruptly excused myself to leave the room as the general tried to have me stay. The sergeant followed me out the door, showing his displeasure in front of the two superior officers.

The first sergeant caught up with me outside and said, "Wright, have you lost your mind? The general can have you up on charges. He was wrong, but he is still a general."

I said, "Calm down sergeant, I know what I'm doing. Go back in and tell the general I had to take a couple of aspirins as a headache was coming on, and I wasn't thinking clearly. Turn the tape recorder on as soon as I open the door and walk into the room. The general and the captain will be distracted by my re-appearance."

"Lieutenant, I cannot do that without an order."

"First sergeant, I am ordering you to have those tapes running as soon as I walk into the room."

"Yes sir, very good sir." He smiled as he left my office.

I quickly called Thibodeau at his home and told him, "I just walked out of a briefing with General Woodcock pretending to be sick. Sir, before I go back in could you see if Woodcock was related to agent West in any way?"

"Okay Wright, you better be respectful of the general's rank or he will have you demoted and I cannot do anything to stop him."

After getting off the phone with the CIA director and emptying the Russian officer's weapon of its cartridges onto my desk and stuffing it into the back of my fatigues, I went to the washroom.

My plan started by washing my face to make it look a little paler. I entered the conference room or what was now the general's lair. I stared at the two officers with the general looking like he was about to carve me up. I made several cough like sounds to mask the click of the tape recorder being turned on, and then I started my rebuttal.

I began with making a feeble excuse of my action, "I am sorry general I was feeling nauseous and had to quickly go to the bathroom in case I was sick. Could you please sir read again your opening remarks, as I now am able to concentrate on your accusations of all who were involved with the latest mission behind the Iron Curtain, and please divulge who the commanding officer was that your report was referring to."

The general said, "Since the report on you was confidential I will not give you the name of officer that chastised you for improper conduct."

Summerall shrugged his shoulders to signify that it wasn't him who had filed the report.

He then repeated the original diatribe word for word.

The general ordered me, "Stand up soldier, and explain yourself, or face a court martial for endangering your team."

"General, the young lady was being harmed. Where I come from sir, one does everything possible to protect women."

"You insolent SOB, I will have you busted down to a private. Do you understand me soldier?"

"General Woodcock sir, your opening remarks or accusatory rhetoric are baseless without any report offered as proof. I suspect you have a reason which is prejudicing this inquest. We will discover sooner than later your motive."

"You impertinent ass! Captain Summerall, I want you to order your first sergeant to hold this man for my two MPs, so they can cuff him and have him driven to Frankfurt where he will be brought up on charges. I promise you right now he will be hung out to dry for his insubordination and the murders of innocent men."

"General, if I could say something in my defense."

I didn't wait for an answer, I threw the Russian pistol onto the boardroom table and said, "Here is your proof those three soldiers were armed. I could not carry all of the weapons belonging to the other soldiers back with their loaded magazines because of helping the young lady. That task was more important than me needing an array of props. Who would have ever thought I would need to prove my innocence in front of an ASA general as I acted in keeping an asset safe. You sir, are out of order and must you be reminded I am assisting the agency outside the boundaries of an enlisted man."

The general shouted at the first sergeant, "Go get my two MPs now sergeant, I am not having any more of this insolence!"

The team members all got up to come to my defense. I motioned with my hands for them to sit back down. The captain was smiling at this situation, making the general call him out for the smirk on his face.

At that moment the captain was called out of the room to answer a call from Thibodeau. In the meantime the two MPs were about to escort me out of the building as the captain came back in and told the general he was wanted on the phone.

Captain Summerall ordered the MPs, "Go wait for the general by the sedan, he would be with you momentarily and then you can take him back to Frankfurt."

We all waited for the general to leave. Instead of leaving he came back into the debriefing to apologize, but still the captain asked him to leave.

The general was fuming and said, "All of you will be put up on charges. It is your word against a general's word that I was out of order."

The captain asked the first sergeant, "Are the tapes still running sergeant as of now, and back during the opening remarks?"

"Yes sir captain, they are."

The general barked, "I thought I told you no listening devices were to be used for this meeting."

"You did general. I did abide by your request. However, the first sergeant was not ordered by you to do the same. Lieutenant Wright ordered him to have the tapes running as is the normal procedure at all briefings. Now, if you would general, I suggest you leave so we can finish this debriefing."

"What about the $5,000? I want what is leftover."

The captain handed him an envelope with a $10 bill in it.

General Woodcock looked inside the envelope and was livid, "What is this? One $10 bill is all that is left. You have to think I am crazy if you think I will make out a report for 10 measly dollars. I will throw it in the trash can before I waste my time."

With that the general crumpled up the money and threw it in the waste- paper basket.

Captain Summerall told the general he had committed a United States Federal crime by destroying a government bank note. With the tapes still running the captain reminded the general he was still being taped. Summerall walked to the back of the room to speak into the phone as Thibodeau was listening to the whole tirade after the phone call was switched to the board room.

Captain Summerall told everyone to take a break over at the mess hall and to have an early lunch.

Summerall said, "It is imperative that you all have a clear mind so we can end this debriefing this afternoon. Wright, you can catch up to the team in a few minutes, I need to discuss something with you."

"Yes sir, how can I help you?"

"We cannot discuss any official debriefing material until we are with the team as you know. I have made reservations for you and Monika on the noon flight to London tomorrow. Do you want to go spend the night in Frankfurt with her or have the buck sergeant take you early in the morning? It doesn't matter, whatever you think is best."

"Tomorrow morning will be best sir. I don't want to be in a position with Monika as fragile as she is right now."

I joined the other members for lunch. No one else was in the mess hall, except for the cooks and helpers.

The first sergeant said, "Wright, how many times have you been told you were going to be put in chains in your short Army career?"

"I am embarrassed to say I can't honestly remember how many times it has been first sergeant."

Back at the debriefing the captain wanted to get it over with quickly, with keeping the conference as professional as possible under the circumstances. I explained how Andrea telegraphed from her position that there was a problem. This caused me to take some extreme evasive action that probably saved my neck.

The most important part of the mission was that the "Cambridge Papers" were taken out of Professor Winters' safe. They were on their way to the CIA's Washington office that day by a military courier.

The captain ended the debriefing by saying, "General Woodcock will be replaced by someone working with General Thibodeau. He was appreciative that Woodcock was dealt with professionally and with respect. The mission was a success, but he thinks ramifications will be forthcoming because of the three soldiers who were shot so close to the border. Also, Wright now has an alert out for him under two aliases and his real name. With the Russians knowing he should have crossed over by now, and being in the vicinity, makes it obvious he is the one most likely to have committed the shootings."

We were all dismissed to get on with our reports. I managed to speak to Nicola, Leos and Kenny. Kenny was to pick Leos up at Kings Cross Station, and continue to Nicola's to pick her up in Harrow on the way to Heathrow to meet me and Monika at 1 p.m. tomorrow.

The weapons were now locked in my desk drawer again; the Russian uniform was left in a laundry bag to be dry cleaned and tailored for future use.

Monika came into my office with an arm full of new clothes and a hat to wear on the trip. She was wearing a miniskirt with a bright orange faux patent leather, trench coat, and she definitely looked like she would blend well in London.

The next morning we left the ASA base at 6 a.m. for the long ride to Frankfurt Airport. I sat up front talking to the buck sergeant as Monika slept.

The buck sergeant was talking about the run in with the general for most of the four hours He did say something that was news to me about a future covert assignment on the border of Russia and Czechoslovakia.

"There is a large city going to be built to accommodate 30,000 soldiers and their dependents."

He went on to say, "The name of the assignment hasn't been determined as of last week. The old man thinks one of the team may go with you."

"I hope he changes his mind and doesn't send someone with me as I can work safer alone."

After four hours of jawing with the sergeant, it was a welcome sight to get to the airport. Monika and I boarded the flight after having a glass of wine at the sky bar. I looked across the tarmac at the airbase where I had spent many years jostling trailers in and out. That brought back a lot of good memories.

When we boarded the flight I asked Monika to sit next to the window. I needed her in a position where she would find it hard to get up and leave after telling her something she may not like.

After we were up through the clouds with nothing to look at I took her hand and said, "Monika, we are meeting two people at the airport in London. One of them is a beautiful English girl that I am going to marry as soon as she agrees."

"Oh Billy darling, I have known you are in love with someone other than me for some time. You never would take me the several times I wanted you to. I love you Billy and always will."

"The other person we are meeting is Leos; he has loved you for a long time. Please don't break his heart right now because you are going to see a lot of him this year."

"What do you mean, Billy?"

"You were granted a place at Cambridge last month to continue your studies there. In the summer you will go live with your parents, and Leos with his parents, as they are working at the same place in the states."

"That is wonderful newsbut how will I live with no money for food or a place to stay?"

"The United States Government will provide you with an allowance and you will live in a dormitory. For this money you will help me by keeping all my appointments and our work secret."

"Billy, I will do anything you ask. Does Leos work for you?"

"I am sorry Monika I can't tell you anymore. Leos will tell you everything you need to know, he will be in charge of you."

"Poor Leos having to look after me… It will be good to see him again. We were so close at one time."

The airplane hit the ground with a heavy thud and Monika grabbed my hand. This was her first airplane ride and she did look a little reticent about going through the door when we boarded back in Frankfurt. I handed her 50 pounds to open a checking account with.

Nicola and Leos were in the arrivals terminal when we came through. Leos was excited to see Monika, and Nicola was surprised as I was escorting a beautiful young girl and she was holding my arm. Nicola wasn't so sure about this scene. Leos hugged me before my own girlfriend did, which was kind of funny.

"Nicola melted into my arms and whispered, "I do trust you darling, don't look so worried."

"Thank you Nicola for that. I have missed you very much and want to spend as much time with you as possible."

Kenny got out of his taxi to help with the luggage as he said, "Where have you been lately Guv?"

Everyone was in the cab as I pulled Kenny to the back to ask him, "Please to do me a favor Kenny, those other two passengers need to relax. They don't know it yet, but they are going to get married to each other in a couple of years."

"Right you are Guv, I'll do me best to git those two on their way."

Nicola and I were dropped off at the front of her house before Kenny was on his way to drop the other two at my flat in Cambridge. It was good to have a cup of tea and relax. Her mother and father left us alone without asking any questions about the trip.

After three days with Nicola it was time to go give General Simpson my report. Our secretary Miss Peabody said he was indisposed until noon. I told her to let him know that we have to have a meeting as soon as possible. Kenny was in his cab outside down the street.

He started to drive away when I asked him, "Where we going Kenny?"

"Well Guv, you 'aven't been to the Russian's flat recently so I gather that was where you would want to go. Missed those bad boys 'ave you? There is a different geezer coming out of the front door recently. 'Aven't seen Aka since the last time you seen him in sheep country. Whenever you meet a new villain they seem to disappear soon afterwards guv. Just making a summize."

"You wouldn't happen to know the new KGB agent's name would you?"

"It so 'appens to be Malenkov, Guv. 'E carries around a leather satchel and I would guess 'e is either is in love with the bag or 'e's protecting it for some reason. The Lambert boys will be on him before 'e's another year older, I promise you."

We parked outside with Kenny taking his notepad to pretend he was picking up a passenger. The cleaning lady was talking to him for several minutes before he headed back to the cab.

"Well Guv, 'e is upstairs and is needing a taxi to go to your neck of the woods in sheep country, I suggest you get back to the general anyway you can."

"I will go and get a cup of tea to hopefully see what he looks like before having to go, and will stop by your motor when I get to Cambridge. Before I go how did the young couple act on the way to my flat?"

"I don't know 'bout those two, Guv. They seem to like each other but not a 'int they would ever love one another."

"Okay Kenny, see you later."

The Russian was out and in the cab within minutes of me getting my tea. He had the satchel tucked under his arms. His profile was almost like Nikita Khrushchev; he would be easy to identify in the future. They both seemed to have the same hair that spiked out on the side.

Back at the embassy the general was waiting for me as he finished his meeting with the ambassador early. He was happy with the work in Leipzig, as long as the job was done he was happy. General Woodcock was being replaced by a friend of Thibodeau and put out to pasture, as he termed it.

The news was that a new KGB agent was now in residence in London. I let the general know that Kenny and I had set up an observation point to watch the KGB man.

Simpson asked, "Did you see him? Your driver takes the embassy's money and never divulges anything to me, why is that?"

"He doesn't trust generals, sir."

General Simpson busted out in an Almighty laugh, but managed to tell me to get out and say he would see me in two weeks.

Miss Peabody whispered as I was leaving, "Would it be alright if I took Friday off to go to the seaside with my man?"

"Go see the general now as he is in a good mood, and have fun playing on the beach."

Chapter 25

The Cambridge Finals

When I got back to Cambridge, Kenny was waiting for me at the train station. We drove to the flat for a cup of tea and to find out what he had to say. He started with how the Russian talked to himself in his gibberish language all the while writing in a small flip notepad, the whole way to Cambridge.

He said, "The man told me to come back in five hours. I ask you where do I go during that time in this 'ere sheep country. All the way 'ere and he never says a word in English not even anything about the thousands of sheep dotting the countryside. Now for the juicy part, Guv. 'E met a dolly bird at a pub and when they came out 'is when 'e told me to leave. I tell you she wasn't from these parts, she 'ad no Wellies on 'er feet. You 'ave to 'ave Wellingtons to drive the sheep. She sounded as foreign as he did as they understood each other. I would guess she was on the game, Guv."

Leos and Monika stopped by to see if I was back. They joined us in acup of tea. Monika was surprised to see the taxi driver in my flat acting as if he was a friend and not as a person who was being paid.

She asked, "You seem to be friends Billy?"

"We are friends Monika and now you are part of this select group."

Kenny asked, "Wot 'ave you two been up to for the last few days, 'ow do you like this place young lady?"

"I like this city, Kenny. It is good Billy has so many friends."

I asked Leos to join me in the kitchen to get some more tea, so I could see why the Russian agent was here.

Leos said, "The student in charge of our group while the professors are away has taken over the monthly meeting, and told us we were to meet a new comrade from mother Russia."

"Leos, let's join the others so they don't think we are rude. I need to see you alone before you go to the meeting. Let's meet at the cafe in the station around 5 p.m."

Monika had enjoyed the tour Leos took her on and did not want to do a comparison of the Leipzig University, with so much devastation still all around the East German city, to a beautiful town like Cambridge. Leipzig was as beautiful as here before the war.

Leos left to go back to his dorm to get ready for tonight's meeting, after seeing me at 5. Monika stayed to cook dinner for Kenny and me when I got back.

At the station I told Leos, "The CIA had deciphered Volkov's paper- work and found out that a sinister plot was being hatched with help from the two Cambridge dons, to have you taken to Russia. You were going to be used as a pawn to get your parents back to their work in Leipzig. Now Monika will be a target when the Russians find out she is also in Cambridge.

"Leos, there is one more important piece of information, Monika is infatuated with me for helping her and her parents defect to the West. I am telling you this because I believe you are in love with her and I am not interested in anyone else other than Nicola, and never have been. I would care for Monika no matter what she does or where she may go, just as I care what happens to you.

"Also, there is a new KGB agent here and he is with a real beautiful young lady who may be a prostitute. This young lady will pretend to be attending the university to get some of you guys into a situation where photographs could be taken for purposes of using them as blackmail later on."

"Billy, I do not understand how they can harm students that have no money of their own."

"These naughty photographs will be saved and used in maybe 10 or 20 years time when some of you will be in a high position in the government. This is how the KGB works, whatever it takes to get secrets or useful information from politicians or government ministers. We have to get back now, our supper will be ready. We need to talk about this later."

It was great having so many at the table for the first time in the apartment. Halfway through out dinner, David knocked on the door and came into the room.

He said, "Sorry Billy, I wasn't expecting anyone to be here, not even you. Why have you come back so early? Can I bring a friend in?"

"Sure, what is her name?"

"Arabella, I met her at the pub at lunchtime."

Arabella was the prostitute Malenkov brought in from London. Maybe she was homegrown and not a Russian. Kenny raised his eyebrows when he saw me glance towards him. Everyone was having a cup of tea with their meal, so I offered the two new guests the same and something to eat. David said he was ready for a cup of tea.

Arabella wanted something more substantial. I had a bottle of champagne that was being saved for my official engagement to Nicola.

I asked Arabella "Would you like for a glass of champagne instead of a cup of tea?"

"Yes, thank you Billy; that would be super."

The closer I got to her with the drink the scent of her perfume got stronger. She flashed her fake eyelashes as if they were fans.

"Thank you love, I have had so many cups of tea today with my auntie who lives in Cambridge."

"Where are you from Arabella, your accent has a tinge of Gaelic in some of your pronunciations?"

"I am from an area north of Perth where my parents' family has lived for centuries in an old castle."

"That is wonderful Arabella, welcome to my castle."

Everyone was now at ease after that attempt at being funny.

Kenny said, "I'll have some champers, if you don't mind Guv."

We were having a party, which worked out as well as if it was planned for everyone to get to meet a new obstacle, or KGB plant, in Arabella."

I walked to the pub where David was working undercover that night. Arabella joined us for the short stroll. When we were inside I bought a dusty bottle of champagne for David to put on ice for Arabella. He excused himself to go change his clothes in the back room. I followed right behind him without Arabella suspecting she was going to be the topic along with the KGB agent.

With us out of earshot I asked David, "Do me a favor, keep the KGB agent plied with vodka in a large tumbler. I need him out cold at the end of the meeting. Arabella will drink the champagne that is bought. I will be back tonight with Kenny to take the Russian home."

I walked up to the flat with Kenny outside standing on the curb, having a cigarette.

He said "'Aving a fag, Guv. Those two inside are 'aving a cuddle. Let's 'ave a seat in the taxi. Now what do you think of the Bakewell Tart, Guv?"

"I think she is going to be trouble for David, he may lose his standing at home if he ever takes that young lady serious."

"Guv, I 'ave run over my time with waiting for the Russian. I need to get back to the misses."

"Hang around for a couple more hours, he will need a ride home and hopefully Arabella will be seen off by David."

"Did you make arrangements for them to get a skin full, Guv?"

"She has a bottle of champagne and he has a bottle of vodka to get through in two hours. What did you think Kenny when she said no to a cup of tea and yes to a large glass of champers?"

"I almost dropped my teeth, Guv. Thinking, I said to me self she is a right one. Anyone could see she has been around the manor a few times."

Kenny and I left the two friends upstairs to themselves and waited for David to signal when it was time to collect the rubbish. I couldn't believe it was almost midnight when David flashed the pub's outside light for us to get Malenkov out. Kenny was fast asleep in the front seat when I shook him to wake up.

"Sorry Guv, just 'aving a kip."

David said, "Hurry, you won't believe your eyes."

I didn't, I was shocked to see so many naked bodies in one pile. "Is everyone comatose or are they dead?"

It took the three of us to carry the Russian to the taxi. He finally dropped his satchel when we stuffed him back in the trunk. David was furious at his newfound girlfriend, who was also naked along with a lot of other students. He took my camera to take photographs for me to use later. We could play that game, too.

On the way to London, with the taxi's interior light on, I went through the Russian's briefcase. There was a stack of English pounds held together by a large rubber band. I took that along with three foreign passports and a pistol with enough ammo to start a small skirmish. I asked Kenny to drive to the Russian Embassy where we dropped the body in front of the iron gate. After throwing the satchel on top of him and ringing the bell, we took off as a couple of guards came out to see who was buzzing them. Kenny turned off the taxi's light so they couldn't make out the license plate number.

I then instructed him to drop me off at the station, and I would make my way back to Cambridge.

Kenny insisted on taking me back in the taxi as his wife would not be pleased to be woken up at that time in the morning.

When we got to Cambridge, Kenny had to wake me up; I must have fallen asleep pretty quickly.

I gave him 40 pounds and said, "The general need not know of your bonus money."

"Right Guv, I don't speak with the general at no time, only you."

David was still over in the pub as I went upstairs to empty my pockets of the gun and money. No sign of Leos or Monika; however, the other bedroom door was closed. I went back down to the street and threw some of the Russian money against a wall, on the sidewalk and onto the road. After having a bath and hiding the rest of the swag, I went to sleep.

Several hours later a noise woke me up with people talking. After listening to Monika tell someone at the door that she didn't see a thing nor did anyone in this house, I waited until the people went away to get up.

Monika asked, "Billy, can I make you breakfast? First have my coffee and I will make you a fresh one. That was the police, they were asking about a loud party in the streets a few hours ago, and they found a lot of money scattered on the road."

"How are you and Leos doing? By the way, where is he?"

"You were right Billy, Leos does love me a lot as he said many time this morning. He is having a walk."

With that he walked into the room with a bouquet of flowers. He gave them to Monika for being so good to him. He blushed when he saw me and started to say something.

I stopped him from speaking when I said, "I would love to be the best man if you two ever get married."

They both laughed and gave me a huge hug.

"Monika, I now have to discuss some things with Leos. He will be able to tell you all about our discussion later."

Leos said, "Billy, I do not know what happened last night. David's girlfriend started touching everyone in the wrong places. When I left to go to the party, you and Kenny were asleep outside in the taxi, probably waiting to take the Russian home after the meeting."

"You are right, Leos, about us waiting. It is good Monika can verify your times if the police need to ask you questions."

"Yes, Billy she will. We are used to police asking questions in Eastern Europe; we just say nothing and see nothing. Monika wants to become a secret agent and work with you. She is always calm and will make a good spy."

I did not respond to that piece of information and wanted no part of such a scenario.

The rest of the month and a half flew by, and I kept my date with the general in the embassy. Attending classes without any interference from the KGB or snooty professors made going to school a lot of fun. Now that March was here and spring was hopefully just around the corner, was something to look forward to in England. The song "Tulips from Amsterdam" was heard everywhere.

Leos said the Apostle Club was planning a big party at the end of the month to welcome professors Winters and Harris back from their three- month exchange program. The venue was going to be too large for the pub, and so would be held in the university's cafeteria. Time was closing in on the group when they heard that the Winters were being delayed because of passport problems. The reunion was put off until the second week of April.

The welcoming home party was on April 13. The next day was Easter Sunday. Nicola had two weeks off from teaching school, so we decided to go back to Garmisch to hopefully do some skiing. We would have to make a side trip to Bad Aibling for a briefing.

Nicola came in for the Cambridge celebration and to stay the night, before the two of us headed back to Harrow the next morning. She wanted to attend Easter mass at her church, and then have dinner with her parents. We were due to fly out to Frankfurt on the following Monday. General Simpson arranged a driver to take us from Frankfurt to Bad Aibling with an Army courier for my briefing, and to pick up the Karmann Ghia to use and return it to Frankfurt when we left.

At the party Stephanie Winters came over and sat with all of the Op's crew. If only she knew we were all in this together.

She said, "You were a naughty boy using our names to get those people out of the country. We were delayed for two weeks while explaining we did not know who used our names and old lost passports to fly out of Prague in January."

"Why Stephanie, what on earth are you talking about?"

She got up from the table and gently slapped my face and saying, "Silly boy, just be careful Ludwig or whatever your name is now, my husband is a vindictive man."

Nicola asked, "What was that all about Billy, why would she call you Ludwig?"

"When I was in Leipzig, her husband the professor told the secret police or Stasi I was a spy. That is the reason I had to finish a job early and my three-month exchange was cut short. I will explain everything to you when we are alone."

Leos and David had big smiles on their faces. When the ladies got up together to go to the washroom, David leaned over and told me I had better lay low for awhile. The girls were gone for a long time before coming back and then all of them wanted to dance.

Nicola was holding me tightly as we danced to "Strangers in the Night."

She said, "Oh darling Billy, Monika told me how wonderful you were to her and how you were a real gentleman. She also told me you were enticed several times to become her boyfriend and you never gave in. I do love and trust you more than ever."

The night was almost over when professors Winters and Harris came over to our table. They were quite inebriated as Mr. Winters had to hold on to David's chair for support. Harris was quiet as Winters lit into me with threats of having me expelled from the university.

He said, "What is your bloody name, and I know it is not Ludwig. You're not even a German. You are some type of spy and I want my papers back you stole while my wife was drunk entertaining you. I am going to have you seen to by some really bad people if you do not return them to me tomorrow."

David got up and picked Mr. Winters up in a type of rugby hold and carried him back to his table.

Nicola said, "You have seemed to make one enemy here in the last year. I think we should go. We need to talk."

We said goodbye to everyone and walked back to the flat with David giving us an escort. Back at the flat Nicola and I went to bed as Leos and Monika stayed up and had coffee.

In bed Nicola asked, "Were you entertaining Mrs. Winters while her husband was lecturing?"

"I was."

"How many times did you visit her like that and did she visit you in your dorm room?"

"I went to have lunch with her twice and she visited my dorm three times with me being away all three times. She left me a note to say when I could go see her."

"Oh Billy, I do not know what to say that would not sound as if I was jealous."

"Nicola, I needed information on something the professor was working on along with the Russians. This was something to do with national security for the UK and America. I am a CIA agent and have things to do that may not be to my liking. Most of the past covert actions were to help people; the Cambridge Papers is the dirtiest assignment I have ever been on."

"Billy, I can't think of you entertaining or being entertained by other women, I know that you will tell me anything that needs to be said."

"I will tell you most everything Nicola, - ow, you have a hard punch."

"Remember, my darling Billy, you have to sleep sometime."

On Monday morning Kenny was at Nicola's house to take us to the airport. I gave him a package to give to the general. He didn't know it was the incriminating photographs of the two professors, which were taken when Volkov was murdered.

A note was inside for Simpson to give the evidence to his MI5 friend to have the two investigated.

Nicola and I landed at Frankfurt and were driven in style to Bad Aibling to pick up my car for our 10-day holiday. Captain Summerall and the team wanted to meet Nicola after hearing so much about her.

After all of the hoopla the captain pulled me aside to say in confidence, "Washington is working on a covert action in Czechoslovakia again next winter. The day before you fly back, we all will meet General Frank Neuhofer here to get acquainted."

I enjoyed the long holiday break, and it was time to spend our last day in Bad Aibling. At the ASA headquarters the wives of General Neuhofer and the captain took Nicola to a brunch to meet the other wives. After the girls got back the general insisted on driving us to the airport, which was an unwelcome change of plans as I wanted my car in Frankfurt. But one does not say no to a new general, especially after meeting him for the first time.

The drive in an Army chauffeured sedan was a little cramped with me and the two ladies in the back. The other MP followed us in my car, so I could have it the next time there was a need for me to use it. The general sat up front so he could command the conversation. He looked like he couldn't wait to get better acquainted.

We weren't even out of the gate when he started by saying, "I have read your file and see you come from a farm in central Florida. We have similar backgrounds; I come from Dade City where my family has several orange groves. I can tell you that a general's pay is a lot more profitable than being a farmer."

He talked for 90 percent of the time, but was actually a pleasure to listen to. When they dropped us off they asked us to stay with them when we came back.

Inside the terminal I told Nicola, "Whew, glad that is over, I need a Scotch, will you join me."

"Do we have time?"

"Yes, we have about 30 minutes before they make the last call to board."

"Nicola, did you notice the general did not say anything about the agency's past actions. I thought he would have since he is a new appointee in charge of Western European Operations. All he wanted to talk about was oranges, cows and rattlesnakes. He seems like a man who can't wait to get back to his farm."

"Darling, Frank liked talking to another Florida country boy; he likes you and you have so much in common, except you are cuter."

"I don't think cute is in the file the general has on me. It is true; we did hit it off right away. He will be a good friend to have in my corner when times get tough. I can see why Thibodeau picked him."

We got back to Harrow just before nightfall and went out to eat with Nicola's parents at their favorite restaurant off Harrow High Street.

After saying goodbye to them the next morning, I arrived back at the flat with a note from David. Monika and Leos were now settled in my place. They must have been in class as the breakfast dishes were left in the sink.

David's note read, "The professors are on house arrest, and have been quizzing everyone within spitting distance of the murder scene. I will be in your class when Winters sees you for the first time since leaving Leipzig."

On the way to class the next morning I stopped to see the vicar of the university. When he saw me he spoke of how nice it was to meet Nicola and to see us in church.

I asked him "Has there was been any bother since the professors returned from Eastern Europe?"

"Oh dear, yes they were arrested and put on administrative leave with being restricted to their residences. However, the Nuts (National Union of Teachers) went to their defense and had them reinstated. They are now harassing anyone they think could have incriminating evidence on them."

"Vicar, could you follow me to my first class to witness his reaction when I show up? Bring your friends the rector and the dean with you. Wait until he starts with his verbal accusations of me, and then walk in."

David was in his chair when I arrived. For the first time ever I sat in the front row. The seats were like chairs you would find in a cinema. As I pulled out my exercise book, he started with his holier than thou racist rant.

"Mr. Ludwig Von Wilhelm or whoever you are, get out of my classroom. No bloody Germans are allowed in here, especially you."

He was so fixated on me he did not see the three gentlemen that came to witness his reaction.

I slowly and deliberately took my time getting out of my chair before raising my hand to speak. He was livid as he came in front of me wanting to strike down with his pointer on my head.

The three university officials I had brought with me came to the front and asked that Professor Winters please accompany them to the university's main office. He yelled at me as he was led away, "I will get you one day, and stay away from my wife!"

Since the class was over, David and I went to the cafeteria for a cup of tea. Several of our classmates sat with us to get some kind of inkling what caused Professor Winters to go on a tirade like that against me. We all summarized the situation, and the consensus was that Winters would not be back any time soon.

There was one professor down, one to go. The next lecture was with Professor Harris. He would be most difficult since he was quite reserved and never looked for any type of bother. He was ruled by Winters on every front, professionally and ideologically. I was the last one to walk in for a reason, and this time sat at the back of the room.

He started the lecture off on his experiences in Prague over the last three months, comparing the communist structure to the present-day English parliamentarian government. His warped view of having a totalitarian force in charge was the utopia of all systems.

I'd had enough and wanted to stop his propagandist views in front of these susceptible minds with only one question. "Sir, if the system is so good, why have border guards to shoot the citizens who want to run away from that wonderful utopian government by the thousands?"

That was all that was needed to send him over the edge and ask me to leave.

I responded with, "If you cannot answer the question, you have no substance to your warped views and have insufficient proof to back up your opinions. If I leave this class, it is finished as a credible vehicle for further education. You are a fraud and the students can now be free from your threats of giving out passing marks to only those that say they believe in your philosophy."

That was all that was needed to have him work his way to the back of the lecture hall to verbally assault me and use a little physical violence. The three officials were again at the side of the room to witness this other tirade. The classroom erupted in applause as Professor Harris was led away.

As it happened, the days of the Apostle Club were without a sail or a skipper to navigate it through the murky fog of communism. It floundered for the few remaining months before its death.

Even though the job was completed, I wanted to finish the year and maybe even come back the next year. First, if I could buckle down and pass the year-end finals, the feeling would be very gratifying.

The next two months was spent enjoying campus life, especially holding discussions on different types of governments.

After receiving passing grades without having to blackmail a bent don was good. We all celebrated the results of hard work. Leos and Monika were off to New Mexico to spend the summer with their parents.

Winters and Harris were convicted of traitorous acts against Her Majesty's Government and sentenced to five years in Wormwood Scrubs Prison. They could have been convicted of treason for breaking the official secrets act and hung instead.

Nicola and I decided to take the summer off traveling to see my family in Florida with an occasional briefing in Washington. Bits of information was leaked that the CIA was getting ready for an operation that was still top secret, somewhere in Eastern Europe.

The summer was spent between Lithia Springs and Gasparilla Island, swimming in a fresh-water spring or the Gulf of Mexico.

Chapter 26

Taking on the KGB

Now with the summer over, it was time to head back to Cambridge and my flat. When I arrived at my place Monika had it clean and ready to be opened up again. She told me all about her and Leos' parents, they were very happy and wished I could get two more friends out who would like to defect. She thought the two in question had a daughter at the University in Prague.

The husband was head of the jet propulsion laboratory in Leipzig and was now guarded night and day.

I told Monika, "I may not do another operation in a Soviet Bloc country again. Going to university will suit me very much."

"You must talk to the Americans so they will let you go and rescue them. I will go with you, Billy, and help. That was exciting last January."

"Monika, having you with me would be too dangerous."

"I can protect you and me if I had a gun."

"No, the danger would be you and me, not the Stasi."

She burst out laughing and said, "I see Billy, what would Leos think or your beautiful Nicola."

"Precisely."

Thank God Leos just walked in, to catch us laughing.

He asked, "I see Monika has persuaded you to take her with you to help another couple get to the West."

"No, she has not and that decision has to come from Washington where all assignments are generated."

"Why not free-lance, Billy?"

"No way, I need a team behind me to provide money and logistics. Each assignment costs thousands of dollars."

Now that discussion was over with these two, I was back to getting ready for classes. The conversation was not leaving my mind as that was probably what the general and captain was referring to, a covert action in the new year again. The communist soldiers would definitely be waiting in full strength close to the border the next time.

The first week of school was fun, seeing all of the new faces who were starting their first year. All types of accents representing the four home countries. The posh affluent accent was my favorite as the girls sounded so sexy, probably because Nicola had such an accent.

General Simpson summoned me to London, along with Leos and David. Kenny picked us up Saturday morning for a meeting at a pub in Ely by the river.

When we arrived, the general was sitting at a table watching long boats navigate a large lock. Two MPs standing by an Army green sedan were drawing all of the attention away from our meeting.

He welcomed us all, including Kenny, who was told to sit in on this impromptu gathering. He had ordered fish and chips for everyone along with a pint of beer. As soon as the waiter saw us all at the table, he was out with our beer. We were told the food was being prepared and would be out very shortly.

The general said, "The past 12 months have been a great success in ferreting out the Marxists, and having the KGB ops in London in total disarray. I have a check for each of you of 100 pounds, except for Wright. Wright, here is a set of silver cross bars, captain, you have earned it and you are the first captain in the United States Army to earn that rank so quickly besides General George Custer."

"Thank you sir, I am overwhelmed."

Kenny said, "That'll be the day, Guv."

We all laughed and had a good time telling war stories of the past year. The general left and paid the bill on his way out. He did say that he would like to visit Cambridge when we all graduated in two to three years.

With the general gone Kenny said, "Don't get me wrong Guv, I can't relax around that Yankee general."

"Kenny, this will ease your mind, he is another rebel from the South, not really a Yankee general."

We all had another beer while we talked business. I would need help that winter to make sure no new communist clubs started up at the university.

I interrupted the fun with asking Leos and David, "Have you heard of any meetings at the pub that would indicate that the Apostles may be starting up again?"

David shook his head no, but Leos said, "Yes, we are having a meeting in Professor Winters' old classroom to elect officers, and since we need new members we are asking for everyone to give references."

"Leos, would you put forth David and Monika's names? We need to change the makeup of the Apostles."

"Yes, that is a good idea. I will also put your name in. They will reject one name as is the practice. With you having lower grades than the others you will be rejected, but will be an alternate as is also the practice."

"Good meeting today. Before we go is there any talk of a Russian organizer coming to the campus?"

Kenny said, "I know there is a new Russian staying at the safe house and I haven't seen the Khrushchev-looking geezer Guv since the night you turned 'im over like."

"Thank you for that information, we are now ready to go back to Cambridge. I might go and see Nicola if you will drive me Kenny."

"Will do, Guv."

I was back in Cambridge on the first train Monday morning after spending two nights at Nicola's parents' house. Leos and Monika were still asleep when I walked into the flat. Monika stumbled out to make some coffee and said welcome back Billy with a warm embrace.

Leos got up to join us at the kitchen table. They talked again asking when I was going back to Prague or Leipzig, just as David walked in and heard the end of that question.

David asked, "When are you going on another mission?"

I said, "First, we have to see what the new KGB agent in London is all about, and does he have an agenda. I have no other missions scheduled yet."

Leos said, "Billy, Monika and I can go to London and see what the Russian is up to."

"No, you two are the ones he wants. David is the only one the KGB isn't interested in."

"David and I are ready for school. You two get yourselves prepared and don't forget to lock up when you leave; we will be in the cafeteria if you get to the university in time to join us before class."

The end of the week, after our last class, we all met in the pub for a drink.

Leos said, "The Apostle group is meeting tonight to elect officers and to induct new members over at David's pub. Everyone here is to go through the initiation, except for our boss, sorry Billy."

"That is okay Leos, knowing you three are members is good enough for me. Will the new members have a vote?"

"After the induction, they will be members and they will vote."

"Very good. I want the three of you to put Leos in as the secretary. We will then know in advance when a new Russian handler will be invited to Cambridge, and it will give me the opportunity to check him and his motives out."

Leos said, "Billy, one of us will let you know who the elected officers are and give you a copy of the minutes the next day or at least phone you with the results."

The next day Leos was voted in as the secretary of the Apostle Club. That would be good news to give to General Simpson, when we met again. Nicola and I were looking forward to spending weekends together and the Christmas holidays were going to be special with staying in Harrow for the week. It was still months away, but fun to think about.

Leos and Monika were settled into my flat. His first day as the group's secretary produced a cornucopia of information. A Russian agent was coming to Cambridge on Saturday on the noon train. The club had another pub in which they would meet him. The old pub where David worked was tainted and was not a good environment in which to have meetings, according to dispatches from Russia.

I was at the station when the Russian came in, but couldn't take any photographs as two Russian minders were shadowing him at different intervals. We had these Russians under surveillance where ever they traveled. Finally, the CIA had its London organization in working order, thanks to generals Simpson and Thibodeau, along with helpers like Kenny, David and myself.

My next novel:

The Spy Who Couldn't Say No

"Liaisons of Romance, Intrigue and Murder"

I was asked to stay in London and return to Cambridge on Tuesday morning on the first train. The importance of being seen in the vicinity of the university early was needed to give the impression that I was not snooping on KGB agents in the area of their safe house in London.

A scheduled meeting with Simpson was at the general's favorite restaurant, which happened to be his namesake (Simpsons on the Strand). We were always given a private area in which to have a talk. He was pleased to hear we had an officer established inside the Cambridge Apostle's group.

General Simpson couldn't wait to tell me, "The CIA has an assignment being hatched was for someone to extract another two scientists out of the infamous Leipzig base. The agent will have to travel with the daughter to see the parents during the Christmas Holidays. If that isn't possible he will have to get inside by other means, the three of them are going to be taken out together. It is set up for you to go in 12 days to cross the border. Major Summerall is waiting for you to show up on a Thursday afternoon.

"Your assignment is to accept a foreign exchange student position starting before the Christmas break. The place being offered is at the prestigious Prague University. There are rumors that the daughter may be forced to attend the University of Berlin. You will have to befriend the scientist's daughter and to gain her confidence for the purpose of meeting her parents. We have a leaked dispatch out of Moscow she will be transferred to a Russian university for her exile so her parents will have to stay in Leipzig if they want to see her again."

All of the explanations on the danger of going to the same place to cross over, time and time again fell on deaf ears, and tempting fate was of no consequence. Not to mention extracting two more scientists for the third time from the same fortress was idiotic since all of my aliases had been exposed. I needed more time to play this scenario out in my mind as another mode of operation was going to be needed.

Dreaming of different types of covert actions was a big part of being successful with picking the best plan subconsciously. That was proven by past experiences to be the best way to achieve the goal. The psychological or mental exercise was a way of dealing with possible dangerous confrontations that could possibly happen.

Author's Notes

L. A. Wiggins visited Cambridge many times from 1967 onward with his wife Nikki, who passed away in 2011. He now returns to his old haunts regularly with Rosemary Egerton Letts, who grew up with Nikki in Harrow. They last visited Cambridge in 2013 and this was when Lloyd decided to write the "Cambridge Papers," as they spent a few days enjoying the town and watching people being punted on the River Cam.

Printed in the United States
By Bookmasters